"I have a job for you."

Jessa turned. "What do you mean?"

"Here, at the resort," Will said. "I've needed to look for help, but I haven't had the time."

Jessa pressed her lips together and shook her head. "You don't owe me or my father anything, Will. I know how hard this probably is for you."

"You're right. I don't owe you anything," he agreed, "but I don't think I could live with myself if I didn't help an old friend in need."

It was her turn to take a deep breath as she looked out at the water.

"Does that mean you'll accept my job offer?"

Jessa smiled. "Yes. Thank you. And I hope I can be helpful to you. I don't want to be a burden."

"You won't be a burden," he assured her, though she might be a distraction or another mistake. It had been one thing to get over Jessa Brooks when he didn't have to see her every day—but now? It might not be so easy to forget about his old feelings.

Gabrielle Meyer lives in central Minnesota on the banks of the Mississippi River with her husband and four young children. As an employee of the Minnesota Historical Society, she fell in love with the rich history of her state and enjoys writing fictional stories inspired by real people and events. Gabrielle can be found at www.gabriellemeyer.com, where she writes about her passion for history, Minnesota and her faith.

Books by Gabrielle Meyer

Love Inspired

A Mother's Secret
Unexpected Christmas Joy
A Home for Her Baby
Snowed in for Christmas
Fatherhood Lessons
The Soldier's Baby Promise
The Baby Proposal
The Baby Secret
Her Summer Refuge

Visit the Author Profile page at LoveInspired.com for more titles.

Her Summer Refuge

GABRIELLE MEYER

LOVE INSPIRED
INSPIRATIONAL ROMANCE

LOVE INSPIRED®
INSPIRATIONAL ROMANCE

ISBN-13: 978-1-335-59742-7

Her Summer Refuge

Copyright © 2024 by Gabrielle Meyer

For questions and comments about the quality of this book, please contact us
at CustomerService@Harlequin.com.

® is a trademark of Harlequin Enterprises ULC.

Love Inspired
22 Adelaide St. West, 41st Floor
Toronto, Ontario M5H 4E3, Canada
www.LoveInspired.com

Printed in Lithuania

MIX
Paper | Supporting
responsible forestry
FSC® C021394

Through wisdom is an house builded;
and by understanding it is established:
And by knowledge shall the chambers be filled
with all precious and pleasant riches.
—*Proverbs* 24:3–4

To Joyce Heffron and Mandy Heffron,
lifelong friends, sisters in Christ and cofounders
of the Mississippi River Readers Retreat. Thank you
for all you do to support Christian Fiction—and me.

Chapter One

A flash of lightning was followed by a crack of thunder so close, William Madden flinched. The wind was fierce, bending the stately pine trees on the riverfront property, making him wonder if they'd withstand the onslaught of the summer storm.

The lights in his cabin flickered and died, and the sudden quiet as the refrigerator shut off left him feeling oddly alone. It was only six o'clock, but the darkness of the storm made it feel like midnight.

Will stood at the sliding glass doors in the dining room and watched the storm as it moved across the Mississippi River, causing white caps to form on the generally placid water. The five other cabins in the small resort were all occupied by visitors who were hunkered down, like him. His cabin was the biggest, since he was the owner of the resort, a decision that still left him uncertain. What had made him think that uprooting his life and resigning from his corporate job in Minneapolis was a good idea? Coming back to Timber Falls to be near his aging parents had seemed smart at the time—but after just five months of running the resort, he was having second thoughts.

A flash of headlights hit the wall above Will's head, and he turned toward the front of the cabin. A driveway led into the property and a sign pointed people to the main cabin for check-in. It wasn't unusual to have people pull up and knock on his front door—but who would be out in a storm like this?

He sighed. Whoever it was, they'd be disappointed to learn that all the cabins were booked for the rest of the summer. Sometimes people pulled off the highway outside Timber Falls hoping he'd have a vacancy, but that was rarely the case. Brooks Family Resort had been around since the 1950s and many of the same families booked their week-long stays a year in advance. But even with the five cabins being rented out, it wasn't enough income to sustain a decent lifestyle. And that's why he had a plan for expansion—if the city council would approve his variance.

Will walked through the dining room and into the living room, toward the front of the cabin. He opened the door leading into the main lobby for the small mom-and-pop resort. A puddle on the floor in the lobby caused him to look up—and sure enough, there was another leak. It was the third one he'd found since the storm hit fifteen minutes ago. With a frustrated groan, he took a potted plant from the corner of the lobby and slipped it under the leak. At least the plant would be watered, and he could deal with the leak after he turned away the new arrival.

Another flash of lightning lit up the sky and was immediately followed by thunder so loud and so close, it felt like it was centered right over the cabin.

The car came to a stop outside and a man in the driver's side jumped out.

Will watched for a second through the window before going to the front door. He opened it, rain blowing against him.

"We're full," he called into the wind, trying to prevent

the guy from going through the trouble of coming all the way to the door. "No vacancy."

The guy didn't seem to hear Will as he went to the trunk of his car and pulled out a suitcase.

Will sighed.

The back door of the car opened, and a woman stepped out. Rain pelted her, wetting her dark brown hair and her thin cardigan. It was obvious that she was expecting a baby—perhaps soon.

How was he going to turn away a pregnant woman?

The guy handed the suitcase to the passenger and then he got back into his car.

Will frowned. Was he simply a driver? And not her husband?

The storm was blowing so hard, and the rain was so thick, the woman struggled with the suitcase as the driver pulled away.

Will left his cabin and ran out to the driveway to help her, slipping in the mud but catching himself before he fell.

She looked up as he drew closer, her dark hair in wet tendrils around her weary face.

A crack of thunder shook the earth as Will stopped in his tracks, his heart pausing for a split second as he stood face-to-face with Jessa Brooks.

She stared back at him with just as much shock and surprise on her beautiful face.

"Jessa," Will said, his voice not loud enough to contend with the storm. What was she doing in Timber Falls—here?

Jessa was shivering, her clothing soaked.

He didn't know what to think about her sudden and unexpected arrival—and pregnant no less.

"Come inside," he said as he took her suitcase, his pulse thrumming as his hand brushed against hers.

She was freezing.

On instinct, he put his arm around her shoulders, and they ran back toward his cabin—or, rather, her cabin. She had grown up there, after all. He was the first person outside of the Brooks family to live in the ramshackle old place. Her dad had inherited it from his parents and had raised Jessa there as a single parent after her mom passed away.

He opened the lobby door and she walked into the building ahead of him.

Will couldn't remember the last time he'd been so shocked or speechless. Nerves clenched his gut. Nerves and growing anger.

"Here," he said as he closed the door to the storm. He put down her suitcase and grabbed his coat off the coatrack before setting it over her trembling shoulders.

Despite the pregnancy, she was alarmingly thin and pale.

"Thank you," she said as her teeth rattled. "I've been cold all day."

There were dark smudges beneath her eyes, and she looked exhausted.

"You're probably surprised to see me," she said as she slipped her arms through his large coat.

"*Surprised* is one word that comes to mind," he agreed as he crossed his arms. "I haven't seen you in—" He paused, though he knew exactly how long it had been. He didn't want her to think he was keeping track. "What's it been? Ten years?"

Jessa nodded as her gaze took in the lobby with its small desk, pine logs and pictures of the resort hanging on the walls. "Ten long years."

He looked from her to the suitcase and back.

"I didn't know where else to go." She met his gaze with

her dark brown eyes. Tears rimmed the bottoms, surprising him.

Jessa Brooks had been one of the bravest, smartest and most confident girls he'd ever known. Even when she tripped and skinned her knee in the three-legged race at the church picnic, she hadn't cried. He couldn't remember ever seeing her cry.

"Philippe left me," she said as she looked down at her stomach. She shook her head. "He cleaned out our bank accounts, what little there was, and moved in with another woman. On the same day our divorce papers arrived, I was told my marriage visa was rescinded and I needed to leave France." She pressed her lips together and inhaled a shuddering breath. "I know I'm the last person you want to see. Honestly, I didn't even know you were going to be here. When I spoke to my dad in February, he told me the new owner promised I'd always have a place to stay, if I needed one." She looked toward the door and then started to pull out her cell phone. "I'll call the Uber back and find somewhere else to stay."

"Don't—" Will put his hand on her cell phone to stop her, sighing. No matter what had happened between them, he couldn't turn her out. "Jessa, your dad made me promise that I'd have a place for you, like he said—but to be honest, I didn't think you'd ever return to Timber Falls."

She blinked back her tears and nibbled the inside of her lip in a way she'd done when they were younger. It was a telltale sign that she felt guilty—no doubt because she hadn't been there for her dad, Oliver, when he was sick.

She hadn't even come home for the funeral in February.

"I'm sorry, Will. If I would have known it was you, I wouldn't have come."

"I'm surprised your dad didn't tell you I was the new owner."

"Always the matchmaker, even until the end."

Her words created an odd, uncomfortable silence between them.

Oliver Brooks had spent most of their teenage years trying to convince Jessa to go out with Will. Oliver was like a second father to Will. They'd gone to the same church and then Oliver had hired Will to start working at the resort when he was fifteen. Will had been in love with Jessa for as long as he could remember. Finally, Oliver had convinced Jessa to go to their senior prom with Will. They'd had so much fun, when Will asked her out again, she had said yes. They had dated for four short months before she'd left for college in New York City—and sent him a Dear John letter, telling him she didn't want to see him again.

And she hadn't.

Until now.

Jessa Brooks had never felt so cold or heartsore. It was a deep, gnawing pain that went to her very core. In her desperation, she had decided to return to the last place that made any sense in her life: Timber Falls. More specifically, the little cabin on the banks of the Mississippi River that had been a haven as a child.

In her mind, she was returning to a refuge—at least, until running into the last person she wanted to see.

A heavy silence hung between her and Will as he held her gaze.

She was surprised she had even recognized him. He'd grown into a man since the last time she'd seen him. His dark blond hair was wet, but it still curled around his ears like it had before. He wasn't classically handsome—not like her ex-husband, Philippe—but there was a wholesome quality to Will Madden that reminded her of home. Comfort. Safety.

But it was his stunning blue eyes that made him attractive. They were so vibrant, so probing and perceptive.

A shiver ran through her, and it seemed to move Will to action.

"Come inside," he said. "The storm is supposed to linger, so I'll build a fire and you can warm yourself." He took her suitcase and stepped around a plant in the middle of the floor—apparently collecting the rainwater from a leak—and opened the door between the lobby and the private residence.

Jessa braced herself for the memories.

Not a lot had changed since she'd been home ten years ago. Apparently, Dad had sold the place to Will with all the furnishings. But then again, what else would he have done with everything? They didn't have any family left and she hadn't been able to come back when he was sick. Philippe hadn't let her. The flight from Paris to Minneapolis had been far too expensive. She had begged and pleaded, but he had control over their accounts and refused to let her buy a ticket. After Dad had died, she'd begged again, but he had said no.

That had been five months ago. Four months after Dad died, Philippe had left her. She had found the divorce process quicker than expected, and within weeks, they were divorced, she had her last name back, and her marriage visa was null and void.

Jessa wasn't sad to leave France. Her marriage and life in Paris had been one disaster after another. Yet—now she was homeless, jobless, spouseless and expecting a baby that

Philippe wanted nothing to do with. And she was back at her childhood home, with a man she had hurt deeply.

Will worked quickly to build a fire and said over his shoulder, "Go ahead and change out of those wet clothes. You know where the bathroom is."

She picked up her suitcase—everything she owned in the world—and went down the hallway to the bathroom. Though the lights weren't working, the storm had cleared enough that there was a small amount of daylight from the window. After quickly changing into some dry yoga pants and a sweatshirt, she looked at her reflection in the mirror, thankful the semidarkness hid the worry lines around her eyes and the dullness of her skin.

What must Will think of her? She'd aged in the past ten years—and not in a good way. The adventurous life she had yearned for since childhood had turned out to be a sham. The past six months had been the worst. But she had come home for one reason: her baby. She was seven months along and determined to give the baby the life it deserved. Even if that meant starting over in her hometown.

She left the bathroom and paused in the hallway, wondering what had become of her bedroom. Had Dad moved things out? Had Will gotten rid of all her things once he took ownership?

Jessa slowly opened her bedroom door as the storm continued to blow outside and she inhaled a surprised breath.

Her room hadn't changed a bit since she'd left for college. All her high school memorabilia were still hanging from the corkboard. A Timber Falls pennant, awards from drama club, pictures from her spring musical and fall play, medals from speech meets and so much more. The white bedroom set her father had bought for her after saving up for two years was in pristine condition. The quilt her grandmother had made for her was on the bed. And her treasured books were on the tall shelf with other mementos from her childhood.

It was as if time had stood still.

She closed the door and reentered the living room.

The fireplace was crackling, and heat poured into the room. She went up to the hearth and spread out her hands, thankful for the warmth. Will entered the living room from the kitchen with a steaming cup in his hand.

"Chamomile tea," he said, "with a little honey."

Exactly how she liked it.

"Thank you." She took the cup and wrapped her cold fingers around it.

They stood for a couple of seconds, just looking at one another. Will's gaze was full of apprehension—and rightfully so. She'd broken his heart, and though ten years had passed, it wasn't the kind of heartache that someone forgot about easily. If she wasn't mistaken, there was some anger in his gaze, as well.

Finally, Will said, "Have a seat."

She was exhausted, so she sank into the worn La-Z-Boy recliner, her dad's favorite chair, feeling like he was giving her a long-lost hug. She missed her dad, but her guilt about not being there for him at the end cut her deeply.

Will took a seat across from her and put his elbows on his knees. "I'm sorry about all your troubles."

He was sorry? She was the one who needed to apologize.

"You have nothing to be sorry about," she said, in a quiet voice.

"I'm sorry you've gone through so much pain." He looked up at her, his emotions hidden behind a reserved facade.

"I would have come home to be with my dad when he was sick," she said, trying to explain herself without making excuses. "But Philippe wouldn't let me. I used every penny I had to get this ticket to be here now, even selling my wedding ring to a pawnbroker. I'm sure I didn't get the best price, either. I could never master the French language."

It had been one of many of her issues.

"You're here now," he said. "Your old room is available for as long as you need."

She looked at her tea again, wondering how weird it would be to stay in the same house as him. The house that was full of so many memories.

But he interrupted her thoughts. "I'll stay in the boat-house. It isn't fancy, but it's dry and clean. I'm in the process of remodeling it for another cabin."

"I can't kick you out of your own house."

"I made a promise to your dad, Jessa. I won't turn you away—especially with—" He motioned to her midsection.

"The baby," she said as she rested her free hand on her swollen stomach.

He looked away from her toward the fire, clearly uncomfortable. "When is it due?"

"The beginning of September." Just two short months away.

Will stood and moved some of the logs, causing a cascade of sparks to fly up the chimney.

The electricity was still out, and the storm was blowing, though the thunder and lightning had passed. The sky was starting to lighten up, as well, offering a little more light.

A bucket nearby was catching another leak and Jessa took the opportunity to look around.

Will noticed.

"I spent the first few months remodeling the guest cabins," he said. "I plan to get to this place this winter—if I'm still here."

"Still here?" She looked at him sharply. "What does that mean?"

He stared into the flames and shook his head. "I don't want to worry you about it now."

"What's going on, Will?"

He sighed. "I bought this resort from your dad on kind of a whim. I was burnt out at my job, a long-term relationship had just ended and my mom was sick."

His mom? Jessa sat up a little straighter. Sandy Madden had been one of her mentors at church and a mother-like figure in her life. Her pulse thrummed. "Is she okay?"

"Mom?" he asked. "Yeah. She recovered. But your dad was sick, too, and he was afraid that the resort would be parceled off for single-property cabins if I didn't buy it. He hated to see the property divided up—so, I agreed to purchase it. But I knew it couldn't sustain itself on the five cabins—so I purchased the adjoining land, hoping to create a summer theme park with a mini-golf course and waterslides."

"I think that's an amazing idea."

"Well—" he shrugged "—I did, too. But the mayor doesn't seem to think so. I need a variance for the amusement park because it's in city limits. He's being difficult, making me jump through a lot of hoops, with no guarantee that they'll approve the variance. I have a lot of money invested in my waterfront property and if I can't get the variance, I'll have no way of paying for it. I've already eaten up most of my savings."

"I'm sorry, Will."

She knew what it felt like to have a dream and see it crumble around her feet. Her dream was a little different, but no less difficult.

He glanced at her, his gaze heavy, and she wanted to

apologize for so much more. But it felt strange to bring up the past. Maybe they could ignore it.

"I don't want to be a burden to you," she said. "In the morning, I'll start looking for another place to stay. I'll need to find a job, too. Hopefully there's something available."

"You look really tired, Jessa," he said. "With all that traveling, I'm sure you haven't slept well in a couple of days. Feel free to go to bed and get a good night's sleep. You don't need to worry about where you're going to stay for now. You're welcome here as long as you need."

It was the second time he'd made that offer, but she knew better.

The sooner she could get out of his house, the better. For both of them.

Chapter Two

The sky was filled with several shades of pink from the early morning sunrise as Will sat on his back deck the next day, looking out at the Mississippi River. The six resort cabins were in a row along the banks of the river, each with a sidewalk leading down to six docks. The docks were rented, along with the cabins, and guests brought their boats and water toys to use while staying at the resort. Will's cabin sat in the middle of them, set back from the water a little farther, closer to the road so people would come there first when they checked in.

This early in the morning, Will was usually the only one awake. He loved rising a few minutes before the sun and taking a cup of coffee to sit on the deck to think and pray.

He had a lot to talk to God about this morning. Namely, Jessa Brooks and what he was going to do about her arrival.

The sliding door opened, and Jessa appeared, a cup of coffee in hand.

"I hope you don't mind that I helped myself," she said as she lifted the coffee mug to show him.

Will sat up straighter, not prepared for company. He was still in his pajama bottoms and a T-shirt, he hadn't shaved and he was wearing his glasses. Not exactly how he wanted to present himself to Jessa.

She, on the other hand, looked beautiful with her messy bun, slippered feet and robe. She had it tied above her rounded stomach and there was something charming and sweet about seeing her pregnant. "I found some of my things in the closet," she said as she indicated her pink robe. "I didn't take all of it to college with me. Nice surprise."

"Good," he said, finding his voice. "I want you to make yourself feel at home. I hope I didn't wake you up when I came in to make coffee."

She took a seat next to him on the other rocking chair and shook her head. "I've been awake for a couple of hours. Still on Paris time. I spent it trying to figure out what I'm going to do with myself."

Will eased back into his chair and looked out at the river. "I've been thinking about the same thing."

"You don't have to worry about me, Will."

"No—but I can't seem to stop." Even though she had broken his heart, he couldn't deny that he still cared a lot for Jessa. She had been his first love and he would never forget that. He'd always known she wouldn't stay in Minnesota. Even when they had started dating, he had known their relationship was doomed. He had no desire to leave—and she had no desire to stay—so they were at an impasse.

He just didn't realize she'd break up with him through a letter in the mail.

"I'm sure there is someone in town who remembers me," she said. "Maybe I can get a job at a restaurant—or the movie theater. I just need something to pay for rent."

"You're not going to make enough money at the movie theater to pay for a place that's decent, and restaurant hours aren't great for single moms with a baby."

She shrugged. "I have to do something."

He took a deep breath, knowing that his proposition

was filled with danger for both of them. But he couldn't live with himself if he didn't make it—and he had felt the prompting during his prayer time that this was the right thing to do.

"I have a job for you."

She turned, her brown eyes studying his face. "What do you mean?"

"Here, at the resort," he said. "I'm pretty much a one-man show. For a while, I've needed to look for help, but I haven't had the time."

"What kind of job?" she asked, skeptically.

"I need someone to help clean the cabins between reservations. I also need someone to keep up with the paperwork, answer phone calls, send out confirmations, check emails and manage social media. I have been doing an abysmal job. I'd rather work on the maintenance of the cabins and the property, but I'm not doing that well, either, since I'm so often tied to the computer." He knew that if she stayed, it would be difficult to see her every day. To be reminded of all that they had experienced. There was a part of him that had struggled to trust anyone he dated after Jessa had broken his heart—and it was something he still dealt with. "In exchange for your help, I can offer you free room and board. I know it's not much—but it's what I have, for now. And maybe it'll be enough to help you get back on your feet. If anything, it'll give you a little breathing room to make some decisions."

Jessa pressed her lips together and shook her head, emotion filling her gaze. "You don't owe me or my father anything, Will. I know how hard this probably is for you."

"You're right. I don't owe you anything," he agreed, "but I don't think I could live with myself if I didn't help an old friend in need."

"We were friends, weren't we?" she asked.

He frowned. "Of course we were, Jessa."

It was her turn to take a deep breath as she looked out at the water.

The sky was starting to fill with color and a guest in the next cabin stepped out onto their deck. The buildings were spaced far enough away for privacy, and there were bushes between them, but Will could hear the sliding door open and the boards on the deck creak.

"It's kind of weird to think about being back here," she said, quietly. "I worked and lived at this resort until I was eighteen. I have a lot of good memories here—but I was never content."

"You wanted to see the world," he said, looking down at his half-finished coffee. "Did you like what you saw?"

"At first," she said. "Everything was so new and exciting—but then, it got scary, and I was homesick. And the longing I felt to return to Timber Falls was much stronger than the longing I had to leave it. More than anything, I want to know peace again."

"And have you found it?" He had been discontented for a long time and hoped she had an answer for him.

"Honestly?" She shook her head. "No. But that's part of why I'm back. I needed to return to where I was the truest version of myself and see where I lost it along the way. Maybe, once I know, I can be content wherever God plants me."

"I hope you find it," he said, happy to hear that she was still trusting in God. They had grown up in Sunday school together and had gone on to youth group. His faith, though tested from time to time, was an integral part of his life. He'd been praying the same for her.

"Me, too," she said.

"Does that mean you'll accept my job offer?"

Jessa smiled. It was the first time he had seen her smile in ten years, and it warmed his heart like nothing else. "Yes. Thank you. Like you said, it'll give me a little space to make some decisions. And I hope I can be helpful to you. I don't want to be a burden."

Will felt both relief and apprehension. He knew it was the right thing to do, but he also knew it wasn't going to be easy.

"You won't be a burden," he assured her, though she might be a distraction or another mistake, if he wasn't careful to guard his heart. It had been one thing to get over Jessa Brooks when he didn't have to see her every day—but now? It might not be so easy to forget about his old feelings.

They both sipped their coffee as they looked out at the river. It was running high and fast from last night's storm, but it was still peaceful and calm.

Will took a few deep breaths, praying that he and Jessa wouldn't regret this decision.

She yawned and he noted, again, that she was thin and pale.

"Are you feeling okay?" he asked.

"Just tired. It's been tough since Dad died, but the past month, since Philippe left, has been some of the hardest weeks of my life."

"If you want to sleep today—or if you need to rest at any time—feel free. I don't want you overdoing it."

Jessa's full lips lifted into another smile, but this one was filled with warmth. "Thank you. It's been a long time since I've felt cared for."

Her words went straight to his heart, and he felt protective of her in a way that surprised him.

How could anyone leave their wife, pregnant, with nothing and nowhere to go? And Jessa, of all people? If she was his wife, he would cherish her like the gift she was and not let her go.

Will stopped his thoughts and forced his mind to shift to something less complicated and dangerous to consider.

Like how he needed to fix the toilet in cabin three and deal with his leaking roof.

In the light of day, with a good night's sleep, Jessa felt reenergized—as much as she could being seven months pregnant.

Will's offer relieved more stress than he could imagine, though it brought with it a whole new set of concerns. Ones she wouldn't think about for now.

She sat at the desk in the small lobby at the front of the main cabin and opened the laptop. Will had given her the password after breakfast and told her how to get into the resort's email. He had also shown her the Facebook and Instagram accounts, which he had started in February when he'd purchased the resort—but he'd only posted three times in five months.

Jessa smiled to herself, wondering what her dad and grandparents would think about social media. Her dad had barely caught on to emailing, though once she moved to France, he had gotten a little better. But social media? He'd been clueless.

Kind of like Will.

Opening the email, Jessa saw that there were almost a dozen unread messages. Some of them were reservation requests and others were questions from guests who were scheduled to arrive in the coming weeks. But the one that caught Jessa's eye was from the Timber Falls Riverfest committee.

Frowning, Jessa read through the email and then left the computer to find Will.

She stepped outside, since he said he would be working in cabin three before guests would arrive tomorrow morning. He told her there were a few maintenance issues he'd address, and, if she felt up to it, the place would need to be cleaned after she dealt with the emails.

It was promising to be a hot and humid day—possibly bringing more violent storms like the one last night. But, for now, people were out enjoying the morning.

They were just two days away from the Fourth of July and the activity on the river was picking up. Boaters, water skiers, kayakers and paddleboarders dotted the river. One of the families renting cabin one was swimming off their dock.

Jessa walked up to the front door of cabin three and let herself in.

It was strange to be back here—but stranger still to see all the improvements Will had made to the guest cabin.

The work was beautiful.

She paused as she admired the newly refinished hardwood floors, the new windows, the fresh coat of paint and the remodeled kitchenette. He'd been the handyman at the resort in high school and it appeared he still had the knack.

Will was a smart man—had been in the top of their class. He was also a great singer, had been a basketball star and been voted most likely to succeed. He had mentioned a job in Minneapolis. It was probably a high-paying corporate job.

But he had purchased this place on a whim.

Interesting.

There was a lot she didn't know about him—but would he be willing to open up to her, if she asked?

Did she want to know?

"Hey, Will?" she asked.

"I'm working on the toilet in the bathroom," he called back. "Hold on a minute. I'll come to you."

She waited, noting that some of the furniture had also been replaced, though it had a flavor reminiscent of the older stuff.

Will appeared with a large wrench in hand. "Is everything okay?"

"Yes." She tried not to notice how muscular his biceps were under his T-shirt sleeves. "There's an email here that you should probably read. It was sent to you last week and you didn't open it—but they need an answer."

Frowning, Will joined her.

She was wearing a pair of maternity shorts and a simple blouse with flip-flops. Nothing fancy or special. Did he think she looked as frumpy as she felt?

Will took the computer from her and read through the email.

He started to make a face.

"What?" she asked.

"I can't be the chairman of the Riverfest committee board. It's three weeks away! And, even if it wasn't, I still couldn't do it."

"Why not?" she asked. "It sounds like most of the pieces are in place. They just need someone to fill the position since the last board chair dropped out. And since you're the new owner of the resort, it should be you."

"Why? Because your dad used to be the chairman?"

"Kind of—but it was my grandparents who started Riverfest to celebrate the community of Timber Falls. Before my dad was the chairman, my grandma and grandpa took turns at it."

"Then you should do it," he said, his face lighting up with the idea. "If they knew you were back in town, I'm sure they'd ask you."

"Me?" Jessa frowned. "I just returned to town after being gone for ten years. I'm sure a lot has changed since then."

"I haven't been to the festival in the past ten years, either," he said.

"That's different."

"Why?"

Jessa couldn't think of a good reason.

"You should do it," Will said. "It's only right to carry on the Brooks family tradition."

She reread the email again. It sounded like they were desperate for someone to fill the role, and no one had stepped up. If it wasn't filled, the festival might be canceled.

Jessa couldn't let that happen—not after it had been going on for almost sixty-five years.

"What if I mess up?" she asked, her heart heavy with all the regret she held. She'd made a lot of mistakes over the years—the biggest of which was staring at her right now. It hadn't taken her long to realize she had messed up by breaking it off with Will. But, it had been too late—and then she had been swept off her feet by the dashing and handsome Frenchman, Philippe LeDoux.

"We all make mistakes," Will said. "It's part of being human. But you can't possibly mess up this festival. It's been run like a well-oiled machine for decades. They just need someone to sign checks and make executive decisions."

"If that was a vote of confidence, I missed it."

Will smiled—and it was beautiful. His blue eyes sparkled.

"Don't feel pressured," he said, "but don't run away because you're scared, either."

His words made Jessa pause and a memory resurfaced. It had been their prom night and the dance was just getting underway in the high school gym. They'd had more fun that day than Jessa had expected, and she'd loved seeing her dad smiling at them from the audience during the grand march.

Will had come up to her, looking handsome in his tuxedo, and he had offered her his hand to ask for a dance.

When she had taken his hand, something had passed through her—like a jolt of lightning or electricity. They had danced to "The Way You Look Tonight," and she started to feel herself falling for Will Madden.

He'd asked her out after that, and she had agreed, wondering if the same chemistry would be there.

And it was.

It had been a whirlwind graduation month and then summer—and then, it was time to leave for college. The last night together, before she had flown out to New York City and he had left for the University of Minnesota, Jessa had realized she was in love with Will—and that had scared her more than anything else. If she was in love with him, would she forfeit all her plans to see the world? Would she miss out on the adventures she had anticipated? Sacrifice everything to be with him? Part of her was afraid she would cave, so she had written a letter to him on the airplane to New York—and then mailed it at the JFK airport without giving it a second thought.

The regret came later.

Had she run away from Will because she was scared? Was that why she was thinking about running away from the Riverfest committee request, too?

"I'll think about it and then email the secretary of the board if I decide to do it," Jessa said to Will.

"I'll help you," he told her. "But I can't commit to being the board chair. I wouldn't know the first thing about it."

Jessa nodded and then left Will to finish his work in the bathroom. She'd come back later to clean, though the cabin looked pretty clean already. No doubt she'd need to change the bed linens, run a vacuum, make sure the kitchen was clean and the bathroom was scrubbed down. She'd done it every summer in her childhood and teenage years. And though it had felt like a chore then—somehow, it felt comfortable and soothing to have that work ahead of her. It was familiar. Safe. She hadn't valued the safety of familiarity until it was taken from her in Paris when Philippe had begun to leave her in their apartment for days on end without telling her where he was going. Or when intimidating men showed up, looking for him.

Her gaze slid over the resort—and she took a deep breath. Those days were behind her. Thankfully.

She focused, instead, on the here and now. The adjoining property where Will wanted to put the theme park caught her attention. She loved the idea of a mini-golf course and water park. It would be another great draw for Timber Falls and a perfect addition to the resort. Will's property was situated on the northern edge of the city limits with the highway not too far away. One of the main roads ran by the resort and would make the park easily accessible. All the businesses in town would benefit from it—so why was the new mayor giving Will a hard time? There weren't many neighbors close by, since the lots in this part of town were wide and spacious—and even if there were, she was sure Will could get them to agree to a small theme park.

She wasn't sure who the mayor was, but she was certain if she talked to him or her and put her support behind the project as a Brooks family member, they'd rally behind the project, too.

Jessa felt a surge of excitement. It was fun to be back in Timber Falls—a community where her voice could be heard and not lost in the din of big-city noise. In Paris, she'd been surrounded by millions—and never felt more alone in her life.

Here, she could make a difference. Just looking around, she saw the difference her dad and grandparents had made in this town. The festival was one of those things they had invested in—and she couldn't see it end just because she was nervous to get involved.

As soon as Jessa returned to the lobby, she pressed Reply and started to draft her email.

She would accept the position as chairperson of the board if they still needed her.

And, maybe, if she started to invest in the community, like her dad and grandparents, her child might be proud of his or her family legacy in Timber Falls, too.

Even if it took them a while to realize it.

Chapter Three

Will was still struggling to believe Jessa Brooks was back in his life—and she was in cabin three, cleaning.

He shook his head at the change of events and smeared tar on the third and final leak in the main cabin's roof. The whole thing needed to be replaced, but he didn't have time or money now. That would be a project for this fall—whether or not he kept the place. When he bought the resort from Oliver, he had bought it as is. But he was certain no one else would have agreed to such a plan. The place needed serious work, and because of that, Oliver had sold it to him for cheap. When Will asked him what he was going to do with the money, he had assumed Oliver would keep it in a trust for Jessa, but Oliver had confided that he was in a lot of debt and the sale of the resort would just barely cover those debts.

Leaving Jessa nothing.

That was one more reason Will felt responsible for her. This place should have rightfully been hers—though he couldn't imagine she'd be up to the task of restoring the property. He didn't think she couldn't, but in her stage of life, she probably wouldn't have the ability. As it was, Will had a preapproved loan waiting for him, if he could get the variance for the theme park. A big chunk of it would go to the park—but some of it was needed for the repairs on the rest of the property.

It was a big risk to take, but Will believed in its success. If he could only get the variance.

He was just putting the lid back on the tar when he heard a car pull up to the front of the cabin. Glancing over the edge of the roof, he practically snarled.

It was Beck Hanson. His high school rival, and the new mayor in Timber Falls.

With a sigh, Will climbed down the ladder, holding the bucket of tar, and set it on the ground before he approached the mayor.

Beck was wearing a gray pinstripe suit and sunglasses. He looked like he'd been sitting in air-conditioning all day, as cool as could be. Whereas Will was sweating from the heat up on the roof, he had tar on his hands and the knee of his jeans was torn.

"Hello, Beck," Will said, trying to be friendly to a man who usually treated him with indifference. They hadn't gotten along in high school for two reasons: they had both been fighting for a starting position on the basketball team—which Will had gotten their senior year—and they both had a crush on the woman who was now in cabin three.

Had Beck heard Jessa was back in town? It wasn't likely, unless the Uber driver had spread the word, but Will didn't even know who that guy had been.

"What can I do for you?" Will asked.

"I was in the neighborhood and thought I'd stop by to tell you that the council vote for your variance was pushed back a few more weeks."

Will clenched his jaw. He'd made the request, filled out all the paperwork, paid all the fees—and they still hadn't voted. He'd been working on this process since late April.

"What seems to be the problem?" Will asked, trying not to look and sound irate.

"Too many variables," Beck said, crossing his arms.

"What does that mean?"

"We need to do an impact study on the neighborhood, give people time to make their complaints known, speak to the planning and zoning commission and investigate some of the city policies about recreational facilities in city limits. Now, if you were living outside city limits, you might have gotten this resolved sooner. But—you don't."

Will took a breath, trying to calm himself. "What can I do to make this process go smoother? I need to start making plans for construction, and the sooner the better. I'd like to break ground yet this fall and have as much done by winter as possible, so I can get it finished early next summer and start making some money."

Beck shrugged, his eyes hidden behind his dark sunglasses. "Not my problem, Madden."

"It is your problem," Will said, unable to control his frustration. "You're the mayor. It's your job to see that this town grows and prospers. I'm trying to offer something that will attract people to Timber Falls, which will help restaurants, retail and hotels. There's no policy that says I can't do this—and you know it."

Beck's jaw muscles twitched as he stared at Will.

They were about the same size, but Beck had put on a little weight since high school. He'd gone to law school, got married, moved back to Timber Falls to take over his father's law firm, then he'd been divorced. Running for mayor was his latest endeavor and Will was certain he had won on the coattails of his dad's reputation. Beck's reputation wasn't stellar. It was one of the reasons his marriage had failed—he had been accused of cheating on his wife.

None of it was Will's business—but if he'd been in Timber Falls last fall when Beck was running for mayor, he would have been supporting the other guy's campaign.

"You know," Beck said as he took off his sunglasses, "it doesn't help to get me riled up. I can make this process take as much time as I want."

Will hated that Beck was right and that the other man had the upper hand.

The door to cabin three opened and Jessa stepped out. Her dark hair was back up in a messy bun with a bandanna tied around her head. Her face was pink from the heat, and she looked happy—much happier than she had the night before when she'd come in out of the storm.

She also looked cute with her baby bump. It wasn't as large as some women's—but it was impossible not to notice.

Beck's stunned expression told Will he recognized Jessa—and that he *hadn't* known she was back in town.

"What in the world?" Beck asked as he left Will. "Jessa Brooks, as I live and breathe! When did you get back to town?"

Jessa startled and gripped the cleaning supplies in her hands. For a second, she looked embarrassed—but she quickly rallied and smiled for Beck.

"Hi, Beck. I didn't realize you were still in Timber Falls."

"I took over Hanson law firm," he said. "Come here and give me a hug."

He pulled her into his arms—cleaning supplies and all.

Jessa glanced at Will with a bewildered and uncomfortable look before Beck pulled back.

He kept his hands on her upper arms and shook his head. "Look at you—pregnant! Where's the father? And what are you doing back here?" He frowned. "Are you working here?" For a second, Beck's face looked really puzzled as he glanced between Jessa and Will. "Don't tell me this guy's the father of your—"

"No," Jessa said quickly, her cheeks turning pinker than before. "I just got here last night, and Will was kind enough to give me my old job back." She lifted the cleaning supplies and moved out of Beck's grasp.

"Where's your husband? You are married, aren't you? Last I heard, you were living in Europe somewhere."

She backed up a little more and it was clear she was uncomfortable. "France."

"Is your husband still there?"

Obviously, Beck wasn't taking the hint that Jessa was uncomfortable.

"Jessa's here helping me out for a while," Will said as he approached her and took the cleaning supplies out of her hands.

Beck's frown deepened. "I know a divorcée when I see one."

Jessa looked down.

"Sheesh, Beck," Will said. "Can't you tell she doesn't want to talk about it?"

"I'm divorced," Beck said to her. "No harm done."

Jessa's pain was hard to miss—it was written all over her face. A lot of harm had been done and Beck's insensitivity was making it worse.

"There's lemonade in the kitchen," Will said to Jessa. "Help yourself."

She nodded, offering him a thankful smile. Then she looked at Beck. "It was nice seeing you again, Beck."

"Hey," he said as she started to walk away, "you're not leaving, are you? We have a lot of catching up to do."

"Maybe some other time. I'm still jet-lagged, and I need to put my feet up for a while."

"I'd be happy to join you for some lemonade," he offered.

"I'll have to give you a rain check." She smiled and then walked toward the cabin.

Beck's smile was bright. "Jessa Brooks—still looking good, even pregnant."

Will rolled his eyes. "Can you be more insensitive?"

Beck slipped his sunglasses on, as if he hadn't heard Will. "This changes everything."

"What does it change?"

"Jessa's back, she's clearly upset about her ex-husband—because I'm assuming he is an ex-husband—and she's vulnerable. This is where I shine."

"Get out of here," Will said, feeling like they were back in high school. "I'm sure you have better things to do. Jessa just got back to town, and she needs some privacy and time to put her life together. She doesn't need you tripping over yourself to impress her."

Beck grinned. "We'll see about that."

Without even saying goodbye, Beck jumped into his car and took off down the road.

Great. This was all he and Jessa needed. Beck was already one of Will's biggest problems. He didn't need the guy coming around more often, bothering Jessa.

Will usually picked up his construction messes as soon as he made them, not wanting his property to look unkempt. But he left the ladder and tar and went into the cabin with the cleaning supplies in hand.

Jessa was sitting at the dining room table, a glass of lemonade in front of her, looking out the sliding glass doors toward the river.

"I hope he didn't bother you," Will said as he set the glass cleaner and rags on the counter.

"Beck Hanson?" Jessa asked with a shake of her head.

"I kind of knew I'd be dealing with my past when I came back to town—but I didn't realize he was still here."

"He's not only still here, but he's the mayor."

Jessa's mouth parted as she turned to Will. "*He's* the mayor? The one giving you a hard time about the variance?"

"That's the one."

"But why? I know you guys weren't friends in high school, but why would he go out of his way to make your life more difficult?"

Did she not know? If it had just been the basketball rivalry, Beck probably would have forgotten about it by now.

But Beck's crush on Jessa had been legendary. He talked about her all the time. Everyone in the school knew about it—and when he asked her to prom, she had turned him down. In the high school commons. For the entire school to see.

"Do you really not know?" he asked her.

She shrugged, her face clueless.

"It's because of you, Jessa."

Jessa stared at Will, a little surprised at what he had just said. "Me?"

"Don't you remember?" he asked. "Senior prom, Beck's big moment in the commons when he asked you to go. Your refusal?"

"Ah." The memory resurfaced. She hadn't thought about that embarrassing moment in a long time. "I guess I tried to forget. The whole school was watching as he got down on one knee, like he was proposing marriage."

Will leaned against the kitchen counter. "I'm kind of surprised you didn't say yes."

"Well," she said, "for one thing, Beck Hanson annoyed me more than anyone else I'd ever known."

Will chuckled.

"And, my dad had already convinced me there was a better guy waiting in the wings to ask me."

Their gazes locked and Jessa held her breath. Had she said too much? Was it too soon to bring up the past? She hadn't even been back for twenty-four hours. But it was there, staring them both in the face. They'd have to talk about it sooner than later.

"I asked you that very afternoon," Will said, a sad smile on his face. "And when Beck heard you were going with me, our rivalry turned to full-on war. The basketball season was already done—but we were both in track and he tried making my life miserable. But I didn't care."

"Why?"

"Because you were going to prom with me."

Jessa smiled and looked down at her lemonade. "We had fun, didn't we?"

"We had a lot of fun."

She sighed and straightened on her chair. "That all feels like another lifetime."

"A lot has happened since then."

Maybe it was time to find out what he'd been up to all these years. Was it too soon to ask if he'd had any serious relationships? He'd mentioned something about a long-term relationship ending, and that was part of the reason he bought the resort. Had he met someone since then?

"Where'd you go after college?" she asked him.

"I stayed in Minneapolis, got a job at 3M. I was a software engineer."

"Wow." She smiled. "I always knew you were smart."

He shrugged and looked out the window. "Sometimes I wonder what I was thinking, leaving my desk job to buy this place."

"There are a lot of good memories here. Maybe you wanted to recapture them." Wasn't that part of the reason she had returned?

"Maybe." He crossed his arms as he continued to lean against the counter. "What about you? I know you ended up in Paris."

She pressed her lips together, emotions rising to the surface.

"Unless you don't want to talk about it, Jessa."

Affection warmed her and she met Will's gaze. He truly cared about what had happened to her. And for that reason alone, she wanted to tell him. "I met Philippe when I was a sophomore at NYU. He was foreign and exciting, and he swept me off my feet." She didn't add that he also made her forget about Will, something she hadn't been able to do for two years. "After we graduated, he asked me to go to France with him. I agreed. Philippe had a great job offer in Paris and we lived in a fabulous apartment. We traveled all throughout Europe on his weekends off. But I couldn't stay there forever on a work visa, so he asked me to marry him. My father was upset. He had never met Philippe, and to be honest, I didn't want him to. I knew Dad would never approve." Philippe had led a fast life, something her father wouldn't understand—and something she understood all too well by the end. Besides, her dad still had hopes that Jessa would end up with Will. "But I married him anyway."

She lowered her hands into her lap, thinking about those hard years. "It didn't take long for me to realize Philippe was in financial trouble. He spent money extravagantly. We lost the apartment, then creditors began to call. Eventually, scary men showed up at all hours of the day and night, demanding that he pay them. I didn't realize until later that he was gambling with some pretty powerful people. He'd lost his job but hadn't told me." She shrugged. "I didn't mean to get pregnant. By that time, we were living in an apartment that wasn't fit for the rats that infested it. I was scared and had nowhere to turn. I was embarrassed to tell my dad what was happening—and then I found out he was sick. There was no money to come home—and, even if I did, I knew my dad would be disappointed in me. I couldn't let his last impression be a bad one." She shook her head, tears burning the backs of her eyes. "I will regret not coming home for the rest of my life."

Will didn't move as he listened to Jessa, but she knew he was sad from her story. She could see it in the way his mouth turned down at the corners.

"I guess you know the rest. Philippe left a month ago—leaving me with nothing."

Will moved away from the counter and offered his hand to Jessa.

She looked up at him, questioning him with her eyes, but she placed her hand in his.

He drew her to her feet and then took her into his arms, wrapping her in a hug that was both tender and powerful. Meant to comfort, heal and understand.

The tears began and she wept against his chest.

He held her tight, whispering soothing words, as she let out all the pain, all the guilt and all the fear that had been constant companions for the past few years.

"I'm sorry you've had to go through this, Jessa," he whispered. "If I could take it all away from you, I would."

She clung to him, thankful for his friendship, for caring about her, even though she had hurt him. "Thank you."

Her tears subsided and she felt like she had better control over her emotions, so she pulled back, embarrassed for wetting his shoulder, hoping she didn't look like a swollen mess.

Will grabbed a tissue from a box nearby and handed it to her.

Jessa wiped her eyes and nose, feeling like a weight had been lifted from her shoulders. She had admitted the truth to Will, and he didn't look at her like she was damaged.

He looked at her like she was precious.

Her heart was so broken, so raw with grief, that she knew she couldn't trust it. She would never hurt Will again—not for anything in the world. This affection she felt for him had to be locked away. She couldn't let her heart soften toward him again—for her sake, for her baby's sake—but, especially, for Will's sake.

Jessa had too many mistakes in her past to tell her that this time would be different. She wasn't good for Will— had probably never been good for him.

She would work for him until she found a different job and a place to live—then she'd leave, so that he would be safe from her mistakes.

But she still had one more thing to say to him. "I'm sorry, too."

"For what?"

"For that letter."

He looked down and nodded.

"I've made a lot of mistakes in my life—obviously marrying Philippe was one of them—but the biggest one I've ever made was sending you that letter. I regretted it for years. I regret it still."

Will was quiet for a long time, and he didn't meet her gaze.

She waited, wondering what he would say, hoping he wouldn't look at her with anger or resentment, but knowing he had every right.

"I'm sorry, too," he said as he finally lifted his blue-eyed gaze. There was deep sadness there—a sadness she had caused. "I could have made you really happy, Jessa. It was all I ever wanted." He shook his head. "I might have my faults, but I would have been a good husband." He took a step back and said, "But I guess we'll never know."

And, with that, Will opened the sliding door and stepped out onto the porch.

He closed the door and, without looking back at her, disappeared around the side of the house.

Jessa slowly lowered herself onto the dining room chair and stared blindly out the window.

It didn't matter if she was guarding her heart against her feelings for Will—it was obvious that he was putting his guard up, too. And he had a lot more reason to keep her at a distance.

She had regret.

But he had heartbreak.

Chapter Four

Will worked hard that day. Partly to keep his mind occupied, and partly to stay out of Jessa's way. Their moment together inside had shaken him up more than he'd like to admit. And the fact that he'd been so vulnerable with her frustrated him. He'd told her something he'd thought a hundred times—but had never intended to say.

He could have made her happy.

It was true—though he knew he wasn't perfect. He had loved Jessa Brooks unlike anyone he'd ever loved before or since. But there were too many wounds now—his and hers. His love had turned to anger, then bitterness and eventually into a dull ache that never seemed to go away.

Now, as he put away his tools in the detached garage and faced his cabin, he couldn't put a finger on where his feelings were. Was he still angry? Bitter? The dull ache had seemed to disappear at her arrival—but he wasn't exactly happy that she was back.

It was later than usual when he finished his work for the day. The sun had already started to set, way past suppertime. The lights had come on in his cabin and he knew Jessa had been in there for a couple of hours. She had finished cleaning cabin three earlier, while he had mowed part of the property. They had passed each other a few times, but other than a little nod of acknowledgment, they hadn't talked since he'd told her what had been on his heart for years.

With a deep sigh, he walked toward the cabin. He needed a shower and something to eat before he'd head to the boat-house to try to sleep. More importantly, he needed to find a way to ease back into the easy camaraderie they'd been experiencing earlier that day.

Will opened the lobby door and then locked it behind him. The desk had been organized, the windows looked like they'd been washed, and there were no more cobwebs in the corners.

But it was the smell of something cooking inside the cabin that caught his attention.

He opened the door between the lobby and the living room and stepped into the house.

This room, too, had been cleaned and everything had been put into its proper place.

It not only smelled like something was cooking, but there was an aromatic scent in the air—like a candle or something sweet.

When was the last time his cabin smelled like a candle?

Jessa was working in the kitchen. He could hear pots and pans rattling and the sink turning on briefly.

He walked through the dining room and stopped when he saw her. Jessa's back was to him, and she was cutting something on the cutting board.

His breath caught at the scene she made in his kitchen. She was completely at home—and for good reason. She'd grown up in that kitchen and nothing had really changed since she'd been here last.

Music was playing softly—an old tune that reminded him of high school. And for a second, with her back to him, unable to see her obvious pregnancy, he felt like they were back to where they'd once been. Before things had gone wrong—before the heartbreak and the wounds and the bitterness.

When he'd been so in love with Jessa that almost every thought involved her. All he wanted was to be near her. To see her. To hear her. To touch her.

She turned and caught him staring.

A tender and uncertain smile tilted her lips—no doubt she was wondering what he was thinking after what happened earlier.

He returned the gentle smile with one of his own. He had known it wouldn't be easy living this close to her. He shouldn't have been surprised.

"You didn't need to wait to make supper for me," he said.

"I remember my dad working from sunup to sundown during the summer months. I figured you wouldn't be in until close to sunset, so I didn't start cooking until about thirty minutes ago. If you need to shower, supper should be ready in about fifteen minutes."

He took a deep inhale. "What is it?"

Her cheeks were rosy from the heat of cooking, and she looked like a different woman from the one who had come in out of the rain yesterday. "Meat loaf and mashed potatoes."

His stomach rumbled at her words. "My favorite."

"I remember."

Meat loaf and mashed potatoes were the ultimate comfort food for him, and he had loved her recipe—even more than his mom's, which had caused some good-natured bantering between Jessa and his mother when they were younger.

"I'll be right back," he said.

He left her and went to his room to shower as quickly

as he could. After throwing on some clean shorts and a T-shirt, he went back to the kitchen and found her opening the oven. The kitchen wasn't very big, and with her pregnancy, it made things a little more awkward for her to maneuver.

"Here," he said, gently taking the hot pads out of her hands, "let me."

She stepped back and allowed Will to take the meat loaf out of the oven.

His mouth watered at the sight and smell.

Jessa started to giggle.

"What?" he asked.

"The look on your face."

He set the meat loaf on a trivet on the counter. "What look?"

"Like you've just been reunited with your long-lost best friend."

"I have been." Will smiled—but her words felt truer than she could realize.

It wasn't just the meat loaf—it was everything about being with Jessa again. He'd been afraid that all the bad memories would cloud out the good ones—but he was finding the opposite to be true. With her in the cabin, he'd started to remember the good things he had forgotten over the years.

One of them was her meat loaf.

She had already set the table and put the rest of the food there.

"I'll take the meat loaf over," he said.

Jessa followed with glasses of lemonade, and they took a seat at the table.

The table was only big enough for four people. Jessa sat

where she'd always sat, and Will took his usual spot on the side closest to her.

"This looks amazing," he said, admiring the steaming mound of mashed potatoes, the gravy, glazed carrots and buns. His stomach growled again, this time loud enough for her to hear.

He smiled, a little embarrassed.

"The highest compliment," Jessa said with a chuckle.

Without even thinking, he reached for her hand, and she took his—so they could pray.

They'd done this a hundred times before—but it still seemed to surprise her as much as it did him.

"Some things never change," she said, her cheeks still pink from the heat—and perhaps from blushing.

"Nor should they," he said, squeezing her hand a little as he lowered his head and said a prayer of thanksgiving for the food.

As soon as he was done, they let go and began to dish up the meal.

Will couldn't help but groan with pleasure as he took his first bite. "This is so good, Jessa."

Her smile was still in place as she watched him. "It's the least I could do. You've opened your house to me and given me a job. Let me know what else you want me to cook, and I'll be sure to have it ready for you when you come in at night."

She had done all the cooking for her dad since she was old enough to handle a knife and turn on the stove. He'd missed this part of her.

"I could get used to this," he said. "My meals are usually a bowl of cereal or a sandwich."

"It's fun to be back home and have some ingredients that are harder to come by in Paris."

"Do you think you'll miss being there?" he asked.

She shook her head, her smile disappearing. "No. I haven't been happy there for so long—I have no desire to ever go back."

"Will you miss your friends?"

"I didn't have many. I went to a small American church and worked at a little café. There were a few coworkers that I'll miss, but Philippe and I did not have much of a social life—when he was home. He owed so much money to so many people, the few friends we had in the beginning were long gone."

Will nodded, not sure how much he should ask about her past.

"What about you?" she asked. "Do you miss your life in Minneapolis? Friends—a girlfriend, maybe?"

He took another bite of the meat loaf and mashed potatoes, marveling at how light and fluffy they were. "I still stay in touch with a few people," he said. "But I've reconnected with some high school friends who stayed in Timber Falls. Do you remember Piper Pierson and Max Evans?"

"Of course."

"They got married a couple years ago and live in town."

"I heard Max was playing professional football."

"He was—but he came home and reconnected with Piper. There are others—some I've gotten to know through Max and Piper—and through church."

"You don't hang out with Beck Hanson?"

"No." He shook his head, knowing she was teasing him.

"And…?" she asked.

"And, what?"

"Do you have a girlfriend?"

He was looking at his food, not sure how much she really wanted to know.

"I had a girlfriend."

"Had?"

"It lasted a couple of years, but..." He let the words trail off.

"Did you break it off or did she?" Jessa asked quietly.

He wanted to be honest with her—even if it hurt and was uncomfortable. Jessa was going to be with him for a little while and if he couldn't be honest, they couldn't make this work.

"She broke up with me, but I didn't give her much choice."

Jessa frowned. "What do you mean?"

"Nothing." He took another bite of his food, forcing himself to keep his mouth closed. He'd already told Jessa more than he intended—things he wished he could take back. He wasn't about to say one more thing he'd regret.

Stephanie had broken up with him because his heart was still aching for a girl who had left him ten years ago.

The same girl who was staring at him from her seat at his table.

Jessa knew Will well enough to sense when to stop pushing him for answers. She had learned what she'd set out to know. He'd had a girlfriend. But they weren't together anymore.

"The cabin looks great," he said, looking around the room—changing the subject. "I saw you cleaned the lobby. I've been meaning to get to it. Thanks."

"I don't mind. It feels good setting things in place again. I kind of feel like I'm trying to do the same thing with myself—but it's not quite so easy to know where I belong."

He nodded. "I appreciate that you cleaned cabin three—it really freed up my time today to get some little repairs done around here."

"I'm happy I can be helpful—the last thing I want to be is a burden."

"You're more helpful than you realize. Coming inside, with supper ready—it's—" He paused. "It's refreshing, Jessa. Thank you."

She smiled—feeling like she had purpose again. What was better than being safe, having a comfortable home and contributing to something good?

Her eighteen-year-old self would have laughed at the thought. Her twenty-eight-year-old self, with years of being unsafe, uncertain and living a pointless existence, felt much different.

They talked about the various projects they'd worked on as they finished supper, and then Will offered to do the dishes, since she cooked. She wouldn't hear of it, so they cleaned up the kitchen together, laughing about the old garbage disposal in the sink, which hadn't worked since she was a kid—and still didn't work.

"It's on my to-do list," Will promised, though it made Jessa feel at home in a strange kind of way.

The stars were out by the time supper was cleaned up and put away, but Jessa wasn't ready for bed. It had been years since she'd been outside, at night, just to look at the stars.

"I think I'm going to head out to the dock to stargaze," she said as she reached for the cardigan she had hung on the back of a chair earlier when the kitchen had gotten too warm. "Want to join me?"

He opened his mouth, as if he was going to say yes— and then he paused, and she could see the uncertainty in his eyes.

Maybe it wasn't a good idea. They should probably stay away from each other as much as possible.

"You don't have to," she said quickly. "I just thought—"

"Yeah," he said, "I'll come out. You go on ahead. I'll make us some tea and bring it out in a little bit."

Jessa nodded and opened the sliding door, happy for a few minutes to herself. She needed to settle her nerves.

Being this close to Will again wasn't as easy as she'd like. There were so many simmering things between them—and though they'd said a lot, there was a lot they hadn't said.

Jessa walked across the dark lawn, glancing to her right and left where families had gathered around campfires behind their rented cabins. There was laughter and conversation as sparks jumped into the cool night air. Children roasted marshmallows while adults cautioned not to get too close to the flames.

This was summer—this was what she had missed, more than anything. She'd grown up in a place where people came to vacation—and though it had meant work for her as a child, she'd still made lots of friends over the years and had plenty of adventures.

With a smile, she wrapped her cardigan around her a little closer and rested her hand on her stomach. The baby moved and she smiled, wanting this for him or her more than ever.

But how would she offer it to her child? This was just a temporary pit stop on her way to wherever she was going. At least, staying in Timber Falls was a start to the life she could give to her baby.

It had to be enough.

Jessa walked down the steps to the dock, thankful that Will had sprayed for mosquitoes. He'd told her earlier it was one of the expenses he insisted on. As a child, the mosquitoes had been horrendous along the river. Now, they were a thing of the past and she was grateful.

The temperatures had eased since the afternoon and the humidity had dropped. Above Jessa's head, the sky was a vast canopy of black with pinpricks of sparkling lights. A nighttime fisherman floated on the current, his red and green lights at the front and the back of his boat the only indication he was out there.

With a deep breath, Jessa inhaled the sweet, clean air and sat on the end of the dock.

She tilted her head back to look up at the sky and decided to lie on her back to get the best view possible.

She'd almost forgotten how many stars were in the sky. In Paris, she'd rarely seen the stars. And, until now, she hadn't realized how much she missed them.

Frogs and crickets sang along the shoreline and little lightning bugs floated on the breeze, blinking silently.

The sound of the rush of water against the dock legs was soothing and gentle—and Jessa's eyes began to close.

It had been years since she'd been this rested—this at peace.

She didn't fall asleep—but she was close when she heard someone step onto the dock. It shook, just a bit, as the footsteps drew closer.

Jessa slowly sat up, chiding herself for lying on her back with her pregnancy so far advanced.

"I hope I didn't wake you up," Will said as he stood above her, a steaming cup in each hand.

"No." She took one of the cups he offered, wrapping her fingers around the warm mug. "I was just resting."

Will took a seat next to her on the dock and looked up at the stars.

"When I was little," he began, "I used to feel so small and insignificant when I looked at the night sky."

Jessa took a sip of the chamomile and honey tea, loving how it slid down her throat with ease. "And now?"

"Now, knowing that the God who created all those stars created and cares about me makes me feel the opposite of insignificant. It makes me feel loved and valuable."

Jessa looked up at the sky, appreciating his perspective. She hadn't felt loved and valued by God for a long time— but she had come to realize that it wasn't because He had left her. It was because she had walked away from Him. In her darkest hours in Paris, she had turned back to her faith and found God's love was waiting for her all along. Her small church had helped, and she had found the strength to get through the difficulties.

They sat in silence for a few more moments, but Jessa didn't feel the need to fill the space for the sake of noise. There was comfort in just sitting in silence with an old friend.

After a few minutes, she finally spoke. "I wish I would have realized how much I loved this resort before I left it."

"Sometimes we don't realize what we have until we lose it. It's part of the complicated mysteries of life." He turned to study her. "You don't need to keep beating yourself up for not realizing what you had, Jessa. At some point, you're going to have to forgive yourself before you can move on."

She stared at him, her mouth parted in surprise.

"Have you forgiven yourself?" he asked her.

Tears came to Jessa's eyes, and she shook her head as she looked down at her steaming tea. "I don't feel like I can forgive myself until I have the forgiveness of the two people I hurt most." She took a deep breath. "One is dead, and I'll never get the chance to ask him."

"You don't need your dad's forgiveness to move on,

Jessa—and even if you did, you know he would forgive you. In a heartbeat. Without question. He already had."

Will was right. Dad would forgive her.

"That leaves the other person I hurt," she said, not willing to look Will in the face. "But I'm afraid to ask him."

He was quiet as he sat next to her. He drew one leg up and put his elbow over his knee, looking out at the river. "Why are you afraid?" he asked, quietly.

"Partly because I know I don't deserve his forgiveness— and partly because I'm afraid I've hurt him beyond the point of asking."

"No one is ever beyond the point of forgiveness. Especially in light of God's forgiveness."

Her heart began to pound harder as she faced the moment she'd been waiting for these past ten years. But she couldn't do it without looking into his eyes. It was the coward's way out to sit side by side.

Jessa turned on the dock, so she was facing him.

He looked her way and watched.

She was thankful for the darkness, so she wouldn't feel so exposed and vulnerable, but grateful that she could still see him clearly.

"Will," she said, her voice trembling, "I know I don't deserve it, but I'm asking you to forgive me for being a coward and sending you that letter. I'm sorry for throwing away everything we had. And I'm sorry for staying away so long. Do you think you can forgive me?"

He studied her for a heartbeat and then he set aside his mug and turned so he was facing her on the dock. His dear blue eyes were filled with a gentleness that made her eyes brim with tears.

"I forgave you a long time ago, Jessa—and I forgive you now. We don't need to let the mistakes we made as teenagers define who we are now." He kept his hands resting on his knees as his gaze remained on her face. "I don't want to be the reason you don't move forward with your life. I care about you—a lot—and I want you to have the best life you can have, Jessa, especially as you become a mom."

A tear escaped her eye and rolled down her cheek. She swiped at it impatiently.

"Can we put it all behind us and start over?" she whispered. "As friends?"

Slowly, Will shook his head. "We can't put it behind us and start over."

Jessa's heart fell and she looked down.

"What we can do," he continued as he touched her chin and gently lifted her gaze to look at him, "is pick up where we left off—as friends."

His hand slipped away, and she was left to look at her friend—because first and foremost, that was what William Madden had always been. Her friend. And he was right. They couldn't start over—that would be impossible. But, they could pick up where they'd left off.

"I like that, Will," she said.

"So do I, Jessa."

Something heavy lifted off her heart and she felt her shoulders rise a little without the burden.

She was ready to move on—to pick up the pieces of her life and see what God had planned for her.

Chapter Five

The next morning, as Will sipped his coffee on the back deck, he half hoped, half dreaded Jessa joining him. Last night had been more than he expected. He had forgiven Jessa a long time ago. It was the only way he could move forward with his life and get past the anger and bitterness. But it hadn't eased the pain she had caused. He wanted to pick up where they left off, though it was going to be easier said than done.

But, he was determined to try. He couldn't be another stumbling block in Jessa's life.

As the sliding door opened, he put a smile on his face, ready to face a new day.

And Jessa.

"Morning," she said.

"Good morning." He glanced in her direction—still not used to seeing her like this. "Have a seat."

She took the spot next to him, pulling her feet up under her as she stared at the rising sun. She was wearing her pink bathrobe again. "I realized something when I woke up."

"Yeah?"

"I have a festival board meeting this morning and I have no way of getting there."

"You can take my car."

"I don't have a valid driver's license anymore. I let it expire. I'll need to go to the DMV to get it renewed before I can drive."

Will had a busy day ahead of him. Tomorrow was the Fourth of July. There was a family checking out at ten and two new families checking in at three. Cabin five would need to be cleaned.

"I know it's inconvenient," she said. "I saw the registrations today and I know we have a quick turnaround in cabin five. I was thinking if we left right away and got to the DMV at eight, I could get my license renewed and then be to the meeting by nine. If you want to drop me off and come back here to check out cabin five, then you could run back and pick me up after the meeting ends." She looked apologetic—but it wasn't her fault. He had encouraged her to be the chairperson.

"We can make it work, Jessa. We'll figure it out."

"Thank you."

They finished their coffee and Jessa made some scrambled eggs and toast for breakfast, then they both got ready and left the resort.

It was nice having Jessa in the car with him again. She admired Timber Falls with a look of pure joy on her face.

Almost as if she was smitten.

"It's so good to be back," she said on a happy breath. "It's like I'm taking a breath of fresh air for the first time in a decade." She glanced at him. "I know I keep saying it, but it's true. I didn't get much of a look the other night when the Uber driver dropped me off. It was raining so hard."

Timber Falls was a quaint town in central Minnesota with a rich logging history. The Asher family had been instrumental in much of that history and their family mansion was still standing on the banks of the Mississippi River.

Parks, pavilions, old-fashioned streetlamps and hanging baskets with lush flowers dotted the historic downtown. Not much had changed since Will and Jessa had grown up there, but that was the charm and beauty of Timber Falls.

The DMV was housed in the large, historic courthouse, so Will pulled into the parking lot and waited in the car for Jessa to get her license renewed. It took longer than he expected, but she eventually reemerged, her cheeks pink and glowing.

As she got into the car, Will frowned. "You look happier than a person usually does after being in the DMV."

"I can't help it. I ran into Mrs. Caruthers in there. Do you remember her from church?"

"I see her every Sunday," he said with a smile. Mrs. Caruthers was one of the older church ladies who seemed to be everywhere, all the time. They loved playing matchmaker with the single people in the church and were the first to volunteer for anything that needed to be done. They were sweet—if a little overbearing at times.

"She told me there's a mothers of preschoolers group that meets at the church every Thursday morning and even though my baby isn't born, I'm welcome to come." Jessa's eyes were glowing.

"Is that something you'd enjoy?"

"Will, I can't tell you how much I've missed being part of a community—of feeling like I belong, and I have purpose. Yes—it's something I'd very much enjoy. I haven't had a close female friendship since college, and I miss having someone to confide in. She said it's a large, active group."

"I think my mom volunteers as a mentor for the group," he said.

"She does?" Jessa smiled. "All the more reason I want to join. How is your mom?"

"She's good. I need to stop at the grocery store to pick up a few things before we head home. You can say hi to her then."

Will's parents owned a small grocery store in town—it was Will's second home growing up until he'd started working at the resort. His dad hadn't liked that he chose the resort over the family business—but Will had needed to venture out beyond his family. Will's uncle was the co-owner of the grocery store. There were so many family members involved, Will had known someone else would step into the hole he filled. And he had been right. The grocery store would eventually be passed down to one of his cousins.

"I'd love to stop in and see them," she said.

Will pulled out of the courthouse parking lot and drove across Broadway Avenue, past the Timber Falls Community Church and to the library nearby. The Riverfest committee would be gathering in the library meeting room and Jessa had just enough time to get there.

"I'll be back as soon as the guests check out," he said to her. "Call or text if something comes up and you need me here sooner."

They had exchanged numbers and she nodded. "Thanks, Will."

"Of course."

He watched her walk into the library. She looked around at the familiar building with a look of joy on her face and it warmed Will's heart.

Did he appreciate Timber Falls as much as she did? Not really—but he was starting to see it through her eyes, and he couldn't deny its charm.

It was a great town to live in. So different from the Twin Cities metro where he had spent so many years working for

3M. He hadn't been as desperate as Jessa to get back—but he wasn't unhappy here, either.

As he drove toward the resort, his eye caught the Madden Family Grocers building. His mom still worked there full-time, filling in at a cash register, doing payroll or managing employees. His dad, too. Maybe it would be a good idea to let them know Jessa was in town before he dropped in with her later. His dad wasn't always the most tactful person, especially when he was caught off guard.

It was only a few minutes after nine—so he had plenty of time to stop in.

Will turned his car around and drove to the grocery store.

The building was old—it had been a grocery store since it was built in the 1890s—or so he'd been told. It wasn't very large and couldn't compete with the bigger grocery store on the outskirts of town, near the highway exits. But it served a special need in Timber Falls, and the individual attention his family paid to their customers brought people back repeatedly. They had started to carry specialty items that were harder to come by in box stores.

Will pulled up in front of the two-story brick building, thankful he found a spot open near the store.

The plate-glass windows displayed the weekly specials and reflected the flower baskets on the lampposts lining Main Street.

He entered the store, the smell of smoked meat coming from the meat counter bringing him back to his childhood. There was so much nostalgia in this store.

"Hey, Will," Mom said as she looked up from the register where she was finishing up with a customer.

"Hi, Mom." He smiled at the customer, an old teacher he'd had in third grade, and waited until his mom finished the transaction.

After chatting with his mother for a few minutes, the teacher left, and Mom turned to him. "Need something?"

"Is Dad here?" He glanced toward the back of the store but couldn't see anyone except another customer.

"He's smoking jerky. Did you need to talk to him?"

"No—not really. I'm coming back in about an hour or so—but I wanted to tell you something before I do."

She frowned, her blue eyes, so much like his, looking skeptical and curious at the same time. She put her hand on his. "Are you in some kind of trouble, Willie?"

"No." He shook his head. "Nothing like that."

"Good." She patted his hand.

He took a deep breath. "Jessa Brooks is back in town."

Her lips parted. "What?"

"And she's living at the resort—for now."

"Oh, Will. Do you think that's a good idea?"

"She's homeless, Mom. She had a bad divorce in France and needed to get out of the country. She has nowhere to go, and I promised Oliver I would open my door to her, if she ever needed me."

Mom was the kindest person Will knew—but she was also his mother, and he could see the concern in her face. "You know I've always loved Jessa like a daughter—but she hurt you, Will."

"I'm quite familiar with what happened, Mom."

"I'd hate to see her hurt you again."

"I don't plan to let my heart get involved this time."

"That's impossible, and you know it. Even if you don't fall in love with her again, your heart is already involved."

"You know what I mean."

"I'm just worried about you. You've got a lot on your plate right now with the resort. You don't need something else to worry about."

"I can't turn her out."

"I know. You're doing the right thing. I just wish she hadn't put you in this position."

"She was desperate." He paused and let out a breath. "She's seven months pregnant."

"Oh, the poor dear." Mom shook her head, her gaze turning tender and empathetic. "I can't imagine what she's going through."

"I just wanted to tell you—to give you a heads-up, so you weren't taken by surprise when I stop in with her a little later. She agreed to help with the festival committee and she's at a meeting right now. I'm heading back to the resort to check out some guests and then I'm going to pick her up. We're going to come back here for some groceries. She's really looking forward to seeing you again."

"I'm looking forward to seeing her, too." She shook her head. "Just be careful. Okay?"

"I will." He glanced at his watch as a customer approached the cash register. "I don't want to be late in case the guests want to check out early. Can you tell Dad about Jessa? You know how he can be."

"Of course. I'll let him know."

"Thanks." He smiled at his mom. "See you soon."

"Bye."

Will left the grocery store, feeling a little relieved that his mom knew about Jessa—though he couldn't shake his mother's concern.

He knew Jessa meant well and she wouldn't set out to hurt him—but what if she did anyway?

"Thank you so much for being patient with me," Jessa said to the other board members as she sat in the meeting room at the library.

"Thank *you* for stepping in to help last minute," one of the board members said. "We were afraid this festival was going to end—but now that you're willing to help, we can keep it going. At least for this year."

"As long as I'm in Timber Falls," Jessa said, "I will do whatever it takes to make sure the Riverfest continues."

"Spoken like a true Brooks," Mrs. Johnson said.

Jessa looked at the clock. It was already half past ten. No doubt Will would be waiting for her. "If no one has any other business," she said, "I call this meeting to close."

"I second that," said Mrs. Johnson with a smile.

"All in favor, say aye." Jessa felt a little silly running the meeting, but Mrs. Johnson had been adamant that they conduct it properly and had told Jessa how to do it.

"Aye," said all the members.

"Motion carries." Jessa smiled as she started to rise.

Almost all the pieces were in place for the festival. The last chairman had done a thorough job, but a personal family crisis had called him away. Jessa was simply stepping in as more of a figurehead to write checks, seek more donations and finalize decisions that needed to be made. She had a list with at least a dozen items she needed to address, but it felt good to know she was doing something good for her community.

As the others started to leave the meeting room, Mrs. Johnson stopped to talk to Jessa.

"My daughter, Adley, is willing to help with the festival. She and her husband, Nate, live on a bee farm just south of town. She couldn't be at today's meeting, but she's available, should you need anything."

"Thank you."

"Adley is part of a mothers of preschoolers group at our

church," she continued. "They're all so excited about the festival."

"I just heard about the group," Jessa said, feeling excited to hear someone else talk about it. "I'm hoping to attend this week."

"Wonderful! I'll tell Adley to expect you. It's such a great group of gals. You'll love them."

That's what Jessa was hoping.

After letting the library staff know they were done with the room, Jessa stepped outside, noting the darkening sky, indicating another storm.

Will was just pulling into the parking lot.

"Sorry I'm late," he said as she stepped into the passenger seat.

"You're just in time."

"Great." He smiled. "The guests took a little longer than expected to check out, but they booked their stay for next year, so I can't complain." He pulled out of the parking lot. "I just hope I'm still in business next year at this time. I haven't told anyone that there's a possibility that I won't be—that wouldn't be good for business, but it's always on my mind. Some of these families have been coming back every year for decades."

"Any news from Beck?"

"No." Will shook his head. "I'm going to call a couple of the other council members and see if I can get them to help. But most of them bow down to whatever he tells them to do."

"I'm sure it's hard for them to work around the mayor." Jessa glanced out the window at the Timber Falls Community Church, excited to attend the moms meeting, though she felt a little strange since her baby wasn't born yet. She had so many questions, though, and wanted someone to talk to. One of those questions was about doctors in town. Whom should she see? She had no idea but wanted to find someone soon.

A few minutes later, they were pulling up in front of the Madden family's grocery store.

Jessa grinned at the familiarity of the building. She could imagine the smell from the meat smoker, even before she entered the store.

Will held the door open for her and she stepped inside. It was more like an old general store than a modern grocery store. The aisles were narrow, the wood floor was well-worn and uneven, and the cashier's counter ran along one side of the front. In the back was the meat counter. People came from miles around for their smoked meat—especially their bacon.

Jessa's mouth watered at the thought.

Sandy Madden was at the counter, writing something on a piece of paper. When she heard the bell over the door, she looked up and her face filled with pure delight.

Jessa almost started to cry at that look. It made her feel welcomed and loved—no matter how much she had hurt Sandy's son.

"Jessa Brooks!" she said as she came around the counter, her arms outstretched.

She wrapped Jessa in a tight hug—and then the tears did come.

Sandy was like a mother to Jessa. As a teenage girl, through their interactions at church and then later, when Jessa had dated Will, she'd shared so many of her fears and insecurities with this woman. And, in return, Sandy had imparted wisdom and life experiences.

"Look at you," Sandy said as she pulled back and smiled down at Jessa's baby bump. "A baby? When is it due?"

"The first part of September."

"Do you know if it's a boy or a girl?"

Jessa shook her head. The truth was, she hadn't had any medical care since she'd found out she was pregnant. There had been no health insurance and Philippe hadn't wanted Jessa to rack up medical bills. When she had gone to the DMV, part of the reason it had taken so long was because Mrs. Caruthers had insisted that she stop into the Women, Infants, and Children Department at the courthouse and see what help might be available to her as she picked herself up. They had wonderful resources available, and they had told her to schedule an appointment with a doctor of her choosing and they would see that she had the funds necessary.

"Well, what a surprise this is," Sandy said—though she didn't seem as surprised as Jessa would have expected. Had Will told his mom that Jessa was back in town?

"We have a little shopping to do," Will said to his mom.

"Of course. I don't want to keep you from your errand." Sandy smiled at Jessa. "We have so much to catch up on. Will invited us to the resort for the Fourth of July celebration tomorrow evening. We can talk then. So much has happened since you left Timber Falls—for us and for you. We'll have lots to share."

"I'd like that." Jessa nodded.

"And we have a mothers of preschoolers group—"

Jessa's laughter cut off Sandy's remark. "It must be a popular group! I've heard a lot about it today."

Sandy's smile was so warm, Jessa's heart filled with affection.

"I hope you'll join us," Sandy said. "It's the highlight of my week spending time with all those new moms."

"I plan to be there." Except that Jessa would have to ask Will if she could borrow his car—something she hated. She didn't like to ask for charity, though all she'd received since coming back to Timber Falls was charity.

"If you need a ride," Sandy said, "or anything at all, don't be afraid to ask."

Jessa wasn't sure if Will had told her the circumstances that brought Jessa to town—or if she just sensed it, but it didn't surprise her that Sandy would know what Jessa needed and make sure to offer it.

"Thank you. It isn't easy for me to ask so much from people."

"You're not asking—we're offering," Sandy said. "It's part of our job as God's hands and feet to meet the needs of our friends and neighbors. Don't ever feel guilty or ashamed to ask for and accept help—especially if it's for that baby. We've all been in tough situations—some tougher than others—and we need each other to get through. That's why God puts us here together. None of us needs to be alone."

"Thank you, Sandy." Jessa hugged her again. "I'm so happy to be back in Timber Falls. You have no idea."

"You're back home," Sandy said. "No need to explain. I know exactly how you feel."

That was the other part about Sandy that Jessa had loved and taken for granted. Jessa didn't need to explain herself. Sandy just knew—understood—and accepted Jessa where she was at.

Will and Jessa took a small shopping cart and walked into the heart of the store.

"If you need anything," Will said as he put some pasta into the cart, "let me know. My mom will probably make most of the meal for supper tomorrow—but I want to contribute something. If you have an idea, I'm all ears."

"I can't ask you to buy things for me," Jessa said quietly. "You're already doing so much."

"You're my employee." He took a few jars of marinara off the shelf. "I can't pay much—but I can offer room, board and a little on the side for necessities. You've earned it, Jessa. Don't be afraid to ask."

There were a few toiletry items she needed, so she placed those in the cart. And she had a few ideas for meals, which Will was only too happy to purchase. As they neared the back meat counter, Jessa glimpsed Jerry Madden, Will's father. He was putting pork chops into the meat case.

"I haven't had Madden bacon in years," Jessa said. "Do you think we could get a little? I'd like to make some for breakfast."

"Sure." Will walked up to the meat counter and his dad looked up with a smile—one he probably wore for all his customers—but then he recognized Will and the smile changed to one of familiarity.

But when he looked at Jessa, the smile fell, and shock washed over his face.

Clearly no one had told Jerry that Jessa was back in town.

Will glanced between his dad and Jessa and said quickly, "Hey, Dad, you remember Jessa Brooks."

Jerry pulled himself together and he nodded, smiling at Jessa. "Sure, I do. How are you, Jessa?"

"I'm good. Thank you."

He glanced down and noticed Jessa's stomach. "You're having a baby?"

Jessa nodded.

"You married?" he asked.

"Dad," Will said. "That's really none of your business."

"Oh." Jerry frowned. "Well, are you?"

"I'm divorced," Jessa said in a quiet voice.

"Oh," Jerry said again—but there was a lot of weight to that one word.

Jessa wanted to explain, but she couldn't think of a way to do it without things becoming more awkward.

"Can we get a pound of bacon?" Will asked his dad.

"Sure." Jerry grabbed a pound of bacon, weighed it and then wrapped it up in white butcher paper. His gaze strayed to Jessa—and then to Will—and back to Jessa. There were a lot of questions in his eyes. "Need anything else?" he asked.

Will asked for a couple of pounds of ground beef and Jessa stood there, feeling more and more uncomfortable. What did Jerry think of her?

"There you are," Jerry said as he passed the wrapped meat across the top of the counter.

But before Will could take the meat, Jerry said, "Are you two together again?"

The concern in his voice caused Jessa's cheeks to burn with embarrassment.

Of course Jerry would be worried. Sandy was probably anxious, too.

Jessa had broken Will's heart and was now a divorced woman with a baby on the way. She sounded like trouble—but trouble was the last thing she wanted for Will. She cared about him—and his family—too much to hurt him.

"No," Will said, his voice calm as he took the meat. "Jessa just got back to town and she's going to be working at the resort for a while until she can get her feet under her. We're friends—just like we've always been."

Jerry smiled and nodded as he looked to Jessa. "Well," he said. "Welcome home. We're mighty glad you came back, though a little surprised and cautious, too, if you don't mind my saying so."

"Thank you," Jessa said quietly, not sure if it was a compliment or a censure.

They finished their shopping in silence and then Sandy checked them out—offering Will the family discount. She told them she'd be over in the early afternoon tomorrow, since they closed the store at noon.

As they walked out to the car, Jessa glanced around Timber Falls, wondering what other people would think about her staying at the resort with Will.

"Don't worry about what anyone thinks," Will said as he set the groceries in the back seat and paused to smile at Jessa. "All you need to do is focus on the path God has set before you. Don't waste a second trying to explain or justify yourself. You need to save your energy for taking care of yourself and the baby."

Warmth filled Jessa and she smiled. "Thank you."

He opened the door for her, and she got into the passenger side.

As they drove home, she realized the first glow of happiness was starting to wear off a bit and the reality of being back in her small hometown, where people would be curious and possibly judgmental, was sinking in.

Jerry Madden was simply the first of many people who would have questions she wasn't ready to answer.

Chapter Six

The smell of barbecue charcoal and grilled food followed Will the next day as he worked around the resort. All the cabins were full, and families were coming and going, needing help with one thing or another. If it wasn't a leaking sink, it was a sliding door that went off track, or a mouse that needed to be caught, or a gas stove that wouldn't light. Even though Will had poured a lot of money into the place, there were still things that needed updating and maintenance. And it didn't matter if it was a holiday. People who worked in the lodging industry worked harder than usual on days when others were vacationing.

The sun was bright, and the air was hot. Children laughed and splashed in the nearby river and boats pulled tubers out farther in the middle.

Will had just finished helping a family get their boat motor started so they could go out fishing. He was sweaty and ready to jump into the river himself.

"Hello, Will!" a familiar voice called out to him from the back deck of his cabin. His sister, Allison, shaded her eyes as she smiled at him. "Working hard?"

"Always," he said as he approached the deck with a grin for his little sister.

At the age of twenty-one, Allison was seven years younger

than him. She had been a kid when he had graduated high school and left for college, but they had managed to stay close, especially when he'd been living in Minneapolis, and she had been going to the University of Minnesota. She was off school for the summer and back home working at the grocery store to make money for her senior year of college. She was an art history major and was leaving next week for a six-week internship at the Minneapolis Institute of Art. This would be the last opportunity to see her for a while.

"Did Mom bring her cherry pie?" he asked.

She was giving him a strange look, her blue eyes filled with questions.

"What?" he asked, looking down at his clothes, afraid he was wearing his shirt inside out or worse.

Allison continued to shade her eyes as she studied him. She had always been mature for her age, being raised like an only child for so many years, surrounded by adults at the grocery store. She read people well and didn't put up with nonsense.

"What's Jessa doing here?" she asked, getting right to the heart of her concern.

He wiped his forearm over his face to remove the sweat, wanting to either swim or take a cool shower. Now that his family had arrived, he was going to try to relax and enjoy the holiday.

"Will?" she asked again.

"How much do you know?"

Allison nodded her head toward the steps leading to the river.

Will followed her, away from the cabin where Jessa was probably helping Mom in the kitchen. Mom used every excuse she could to feed her family and she loved holidays most of all. There would be enough food for the entire resort tonight if his mother had her way. No doubt she and Jessa were catching up already.

Allison was shorter than Will, but she shared his blue eyes and blond hair. Those were the only similarities that marked them as siblings. His sister had always been cute and popular with friends, though she had not dated much.

She sat on the top step and motioned for him to sit next to her. "I have a feeling it's going to take me a little bit of time to pull information out of you, so you might as well get comfortable."

"There's nothing to tell."

She gave him a look.

He sighed and took the seat next to her.

The wood step was warm against his thighs as he leaned forward and rested his elbows on his knees. "I'm hot and sweaty," he told his sister. "Can't this conversation wait until I've had a chance to at least shower?"

"I want to know what I need to know before the evening progresses much further. Jessa Brooks is back. She's divorced and pregnant. And you didn't bother to tell Mom until yesterday—and she didn't mention it to me until right before we pulled up to the resort. Why did you wait to tell me?"

"I didn't tell you at all."

She pursed her lips and raised an eyebrow. "Exactly. But, I'm ready to hear it. Are you two *involved* again? Mom says no. Dad says yes."

Will shook his head and looked out at the river. "No. We're not *involved*. I'm just helping an old friend. And you don't need to lecture me, Allison. Mom already warned me—though I didn't need any warning—to be careful."

"Oh, it's too late for that," Allison said, shaking her head. "I was only a kid when you two dated, but I wasn't blind.

The way you felt for her couldn't be easily forgotten. I'm sure that the second she showed up again, your feelings returned with vengeance."

"You're making more out of this than necessary."

"Am I?" She tilted her head. "You two have been thrown together again. You're single. She's single. It's only a matter of time."

"Allison." He said her name a little louder and more forcefully than he intended, so he backed off a bit. This time, he spoke quieter. "Jessa Brooks just got out of a difficult marriage. She's pregnant with another man's child. And—I can't stress this enough—I will never let myself fall in love with her again. She hurt me too deeply. There are wounds that will never heal between us. I know you're concerned—or whatever this is—but you have nothing to worry about."

"I'm not worried, Will." She frowned. "I'm hopeful."

His first inclination was to roll his eyes—but he settled for shaking his head. "You've got to be kidding me."

"Come on," she said, grabbing his upper arm and shaking him. "She's single. You're single. You loved her once—you probably still do—don't be foolish. Sweep her off her feet. Reclaim the romance you once had. I know you're a romantic guy at heart and that it's crossed your mind several times in the past seventy-two hours. I'm sure you're fighting your attraction to her constant—"

"Allison, the only romantic person here is you. I'm going inside to take a shower." He stood and looked down at her. "I don't want you meddling in any of this. Neither Jessa nor I are in a place to even consider romance—and the last thing I would do is put myself in a position to be hurt again. Because that's what Jessa does. She hurts people."

The words came out before he knew what he was saying, and he paused.

Did he really believe what he'd just said?

Allison frowned up at him.

And Will realized that he did believe it. Jessa had hurt a lot of people—including him and her father. He said he forgave her—and he did—but he couldn't find a way to trust that she wasn't going to hurt him or his family again.

Which was the biggest reason he was keeping Jessa Brooks at a distance.

"I gotta get changed," Will mumbled as he walked away from his sister.

"Hey, Will," Allison said.

He turned back and looked at her.

"Don't let fear get in the way of happiness. Use caution—but don't be foolish. There is not a cruel or unkind bone in Jessa's body. There are reasons for what happened. You know that as much as I do."

Will wasn't ready to even think about moving on or trusting Jessa with his heart again. She'd been out of his life for ten years, back in it for three days—and his little sister expected him to fall head over heels in love with her again?

He walked across the lawn and opened the sliding door into his cabin. He was immediately greeted by the cold air-conditioning and the smell of something savory.

His stomach rumbled as he tried to push aside Allison's conversation. He didn't want to think about any of it right now.

Will could partially see his dad sitting in the living room with a newspaper, though he wasn't within hearing distance unless Will shouted.

Mom was in the kitchen with Jessa, sharing a serious, quiet conversation as Mom made a marinade and Jessa mixed some kind of dessert.

"I didn't have a mother growing up," Jessa said, "and there was no one to ask about—"

They both looked up at his arrival, their conversation stalling midsentence.

"Sorry," Will said, sensing that Jessa had been about to say something she probably didn't want him to hear. He pointed toward the back of the house as he moved through the dining room. "I'm taking a shower."

Jessa's cheeks were pink as she looked down at the dessert she was making. Mom simply smiled and nodded.

As Will moved through, and was on the other side of the wall, he heard his mom say, "Every woman needs someone to confide in, Jessa. You are always welcome to come to me. I might not have all the answers, but I can listen."

"Thank you, Sandy. I know I hurt you when—"

"No," Mom said, and Will could imagine his mom putting her hand on Jessa's. "I hurt *for* you and Will, Jessa. That's different than being hurt *by* you."

Will inhaled a deep breath.

Maybe Jessa hadn't hurt his mom, but she had hurt him. And maybe it wouldn't be as easy as he thought to get over it.

Especially when it seemed like no one would let him forget.

Jessa hadn't laughed this hard or for this long in years. She laid her hand on her swollen stomach and shook her head as Jerry finished a story about a chipmunk that had gotten into the grocery store. Two employees and a customer had chased it up and down each aisle as it frightened the other customers and left a trail of disrupted shelves in its wake. The way Jerry told the story made it come alive to Jessa and she could imagine the chaos that had ensued.

"Needless to say," Jerry finished, "it was the most exciting visitor we've had in the store since Congressman Johnson stopped by on his campaign trail last fall."

Sandy, Will, Allison and Jessa continued to laugh as Jerry made a face to mimic the chipmunk.

A gentle breeze blew across the back deck where they sat enjoying the last remaining minutes of daylight. The cheesecake Jessa had made was sitting on the table next to the cherry pie that Sandy had brought and the brownies that Jerry had baked. There had been too much food, like Will had predicted, but Jessa had taken a bit of each of it, reminiscing about past holidays and gatherings on this very deck.

"The fireworks will start soon," Will said as their laughter died down. "How about we take out the pontoon to watch them from the river?"

"That sounds like a good plan." Sandy rose from her chair to start clearing the table.

"Leave it," Jessa told her with a smile as she put her hand on the dish Sandy had grabbed. "You made most of the meal. Let us clean it up."

"You helped," Sandy reminded her.

"Then I'll do it," Will told them as he rose next.

"I'll help," Jessa said. "Enjoy the evening, Sandy. You and Jerry were working all morning at the store. You should rest and put your feet up."

"All of us worked today," Sandy said. "We'll all clean up. Come on, Jerry."

Jerry sighed and pushed away from the table.

Soon, the dishes were brought into the kitchen, and everything was cleaned and put away.

"I'll leave out a few snacks," Sandy said with a twinkle in her eye. "In case anyone gets hungry."

"I don't think I'll be hungry until Labor Day," Will said as he put his hand on his stomach. "There's always too much food, Mom."

"There's never such a thing as too much food."

There was more laughter all around as Jessa grabbed her cardigan and followed everyone outside.

The first star appeared on the horizon as dozens of other boats started to make their way onto the river. Fireworks from one of the parks in downtown Timber Falls would be visible from the water. When Jessa was young, she and her dad would go out alone in a small rowboat and watch them together.

She missed her dad, more now than ever. Being back at the resort brought his memory alive in ways she hadn't experienced in Paris. It was bittersweet to feel so close to him—yet to not have him where it felt natural for him to be.

Jessa wasn't doing a very good job hiding her feelings, because Will glanced at her as the others went ahead to the steps leading down to the water.

"Everything okay?" he asked.

She looked up at him and tried to smile. He didn't owe her this home or time with his family, but he was letting her be a part of it all again. She didn't want him to think she was sad or ungrateful. "I'm just missing my dad a little more than usual tonight."

"I have moments like that, too, when I expect to see him walk around a building with a hammer and a ladder in hand. Or when I think of something I want to ask him or tell him. Then it just kind of hits me all over again that he's gone."

Jessa pressed her lips together and nodded, trying not to cry.

"It's okay to grieve, Jessa," Will said as he stopped near the top of the steps. "There's no right or wrong way to go about it. Your dad is gone—but all the best parts of him are still here with us. In you. In me. In this resort and in this community. He gave of himself freely and what he gave will never be lost."

His words comforted her and felt like a buoy of hope to grasp in this uncertain time. "Thank you."

Will smiled at her. "I'm happy you're here to enjoy this with us, Jessa. I think your dad would be happy, too."

"I know he would be."

He motioned for her to walk ahead of him down the steps and they were soon on the dock.

Jerry was already getting the pontoon ready to take out onto the water while Sandy was busy pulling life jackets out of the storage areas under the seats to have them ready in case of an emergency, and Allison was making herself comfortable on the front bench. She put her feet up and took the whole space to herself.

Will helped Jessa onto the pontoon while it was still on the boatlift and then he pressed a button to lower it into the water.

Soon, it was floating, and Jerry put the motor down and Will flipped the ignition switch to start the propeller.

Jessa took a seat on the back bench while Sandy sat in the chair next to the driver's seat.

"Let me drive," Jerry said to his son. "I haven't had the pleasure in a long time—and I like sitting next to your mom."

"Sure." Will let his dad take over and then stood for a second. He could either force Allison to move her feet off the bench and sit next to her—or he could sit with Jessa on the back bench.

Allison looked up at him with a cheeky grin and he shook his head.

What was that about?

Jessa glanced away, not wanting to seem eager to have him sit with her—yet, there was a part of her that wanted him close. She felt safe with Will nearby—a feeling she hadn't experienced in France for years. Not only did she feel safe, but she loved talking to him. His calm, steady presence made her feel calm and steady, too.

Finally, Will moved to the back seat and looked down at her. "Mind if I sit here?"

She shook her head and moved over to allow him a little more space—and she didn't miss the look that Sandy and Jerry shared. A bit concerned, a bit curious, a bit apprehensive.

Or the gleeful look Allison kept all to herself.

Jessa hated to be the cause of any anxiety Will's family might have—or false hope. She loved them all too much.

As soon as she was able, she would find her own place and put their fears to rest.

Jerry moved the pontoon out onto the open water and found a spot in the middle of the river with a great view of the park in the distance. He lowered the anchor so they wouldn't float away.

"How is the variance coming for the park?" Allison asked from her spot in the front of the pontoon.

Will let out a frustrated sigh and Jessa studied him in the dying light.

"It's not going well," he said. "All I need to do is convince Beck Hanson—but I can't be in the same space as him and not lose my cool. And I know he loves it, too."

"Some people seek political positions to help and to serve," Jerry said. "Others want the power and authority that comes with it. I've known Beck his whole life and if I had to guess, I'd say he's the latter type."

"You can't play into their power struggle," Sandy added. "You'll never get anywhere. You have to appeal to their ego."

Will glanced out at the water and shook his head. "I can't stroke his ego. It goes against everything I believe in and stand for."

"If you don't," Allison said, "you'll have to sell the resort. You don't have many options."

The first fireworks lit up the evening sky, reflecting bright red, white and blue on the ripples of water. A hush fell over the boat and all eyes looked toward the south.

But Jessa's thoughts weren't on the fireworks or the Fourth of July celebration—all she could think about was helping Will—and, in a way, helping her dad. Her dad would want to know that the resort was in good, capable hands. He was resting in peace knowing Will had taken over. She would hate to dishonor his memory by seeing the resort parceled off or destroyed completely.

Maybe Will couldn't appeal to Beck's pride—but Jessa could. She wouldn't manipulate Beck or do anything to trick him, but perhaps she could convince him that letting Will have the variance would make him look good. And, if Beck believed something would make him look good, then he'd be more apt to let it happen.

Tomorrow, Jessa would contact Beck and ask to see him. She wasn't sure how she would do it without Will knowing—because she had a feeling he'd try to stop her—but she would make it happen.

Will deserved nothing less.

Chapter Seven

A̶ll the guests were staying through the holiday weekend, so there was no cleaning to be done the next day. Jessa spent the morning after the Fourth of July working on email correspondence and Riverfest responsibilities, while Will was doing odd jobs around the resort. Right after breakfast, he had started to clean all the windows in the main cabin and then he had been touching up the paint on the sign out front.

Did he ever rest? No doubt he wanted to hire more employees, but the resort made just enough to pay the bills—and maybe not even that much since he had the additional riverfront property adjacent to the resort. If he could build the amusement park, there would be more revenue and the opportunity to hire help.

Ever since their pontoon ride the night before, all Jessa could think about was convincing Beck to give Will the variance. But how? Come right out and ask him? Convince him that it was his idea?

Either way, it would mean seeing Beck again and Jessa wasn't sure if she was up for it. She didn't want to mislead Beck—but how would she ask to see him without getting his hopes up? Because he had made it clear in their brief encounter that he was still very much interested.

Will entered the lobby with his empty water bottle in

hand and their gazes met. They hadn't talked since breakfast, though Jessa had been aware of almost every move he made on the resort. All the windows in the cabin made it easy to keep an eye on things—which was nice for the owner. And nice for Jessa, who didn't mind keeping an eye on Will.

"Hey," he said as he closed the door behind him, a handsome smile on his face. "Sometimes it still takes me by surprise to see you in this house again."

The way he said it, his voice full of pleasure, sent a thrill up Jessa's spine and she returned the smile.

"It's nice," he said.

Her cheeks grew warm, and she tried to remember what she had been doing before he came in.

Oh—Beck.

"Do you mind if I borrow your car for a little bit this afternoon?"

He studied her for a second, as if he wanted to ask her why she needed it, but then seemed to decide not to pry. "Sure. I don't think I'll need it. I'm hoping to finish work a little early today and go fishing for a while this afternoon." He paused and then said, "Would you like to join me? I remember how much you liked fishing."

"Dad liked fishing," she corrected, her voice gentle. "And I liked being with my dad."

"Oh." He glanced down at his water bottle. "Then I guess that's a no."

Jessa hadn't enjoyed fishing much when she was younger—but she had liked being in the boat with a good book in her dad's company. And the thought of being in a boat with Will's company seemed just as pleasant.

"I'd love to go fishing with you, Will," she said, feeling a little shy.

He returned his gaze to her face. "Really?"

She nodded.

"Okay. I'll get the boat and the fishing gear ready for when you get back from your errands."

His excitement was almost childlike, and Jessa was happy she said she would go with him. He didn't take much time off from work, so this was a special occasion.

"I'll get my errands done as soon as I can and come home and make a picnic supper," she told him, feeling just as excited and eager to get her distasteful task done. "We can eat it in the boat."

He grinned. "The car keys are on the key hook where your dad used to keep his."

"Thanks."

Will left to refill his water bottle and Jessa grabbed her purse and the keys to Will's car.

She left the resort feeling ready to tackle the situation with Beck. Though she wasn't sure where to find him. It was Friday, the day after the Fourth of July, but perhaps he would be at his office. If not, then maybe there would be an assistant who could help her find a way to contact him.

Jessa remembered where Beck's father's law firm was located downtown and found a spot to park. It was hard to tell if the place was open since it was a nondescript building.

Would Beck be upset that she hadn't made an appointment?

It was too late to worry about that now.

Jessa pushed open the heavy glass door and entered the cool building.

Just like most of the buildings in downtown Timber Falls, this one was old. It was brick and probably built near the turn of the twentieth century. Thick, wavy glass windows fronted Main Street and looked across the road toward the Maddens' grocery store.

Until now, Jessa hadn't been concerned about the Maddens seeing her enter Beck's law office—but now she was a little worried. What would they think? Would they tell Will? And, if they did, what would it matter? She could tell Will herself, though she was certain he wouldn't want her to meddle. Hopefully she could get in, talk to Beck, convince him, then leave and not need to tell Will that she was involved.

The law office was decorated in dark wood paneling, rich green wallpaper and leather furniture. A secretary sat at the front desk and smiled at Jessa when she looked up.

"Hello," the woman said. "I'm Clarice. May I help you?"

Jessa returned the smile. "I'm wondering if I could speak to Mr. Hanson. If he's not here, I can always—"

"Do you have an appointment?" Clarice asked.

"No. Beck is an old friend, and I wasn't sure if he was here—I can make an appointment, if I need to, and come back a different day."

"Mr. Hanson is here," Clarice said. "I can ask him if he has time to see you. May I ask your name?"

Jessa hadn't anticipated it would be so easy. "Yes—I'm Jessa Brooks."

"One moment, Ms. Brooks." Clarice lifted the phone and pressed a button. A second later she said, "There is a Jessa Brooks to see you. Shall I send her— Yes, of course."

Clarice hung up the phone and said, "Mr. Hanson told me to send you right in." She stood and motioned for Jessa to follow her down a hallway to the door at the end.

The placard on the door said Beck Hanson.

This was the place.

As Clarice opened the door, Jessa took a deep breath.

"Jessa!" Beck said as he came around his large desk while she walked into the room. He was wearing a three-piece suit and his hair was combed to perfection. In this office, he seemed taller and broader than usual—more commanding. "This is a surprise."

Clarice smiled and left Jessa with Beck.

Beck closed the door behind Jessa, forcing her farther into his office.

She moved away from him, glancing at the tall bookshelves, potted plants and pictures of Beck with various political celebrities on the wall.

"To what do I owe this pleasure?" Beck asked as he approached Jessa. "Couldn't stop thinking about me after we ran into each other at the resort?"

Jessa tried to hide her dislike of Beck. He hadn't changed much since high school. If anything, he seemed even more overly confident and arrogant.

"I wanted to chat with you about a few things," she said.

"Oh? Legal matters? I was wondering if you would need help with your international divorce or citizenship status."

"Nothing like that." Thankfully, all of that had been cleared up before she left France. She put her hand on her stomach and nodded at a chair. "May I have a seat?"

Anything to get him back to his side of the desk and give her some space.

"Of course. Where are my manners?" Beck pulled out the chair for her.

Jessa took a seat. But instead of returning to the other side of the desk, Beck sat in the chair next to her—much closer than necessary. His knees brushed against hers.

She tried to scoot back as far as she could on her chair and devise a way to bring up the variance without it being too obvious.

"It's an impressive feat to become mayor," she started, trying to appeal to his ego. "Are you enjoying the job?"

He lifted a shoulder. "It's fine—for now."

"Do you have higher political aspirations?"

"Doesn't everyone?"

She frowned. "No."

Beck grinned. "I'm only teasing. Yes—I hope to run for state senate one day and then maybe US representative. Who knows. Maybe I'll be president one day."

Jessa tried not to let a shiver pass through her spine. Beck for president? She couldn't imagine.

"Did you come here to talk about my political aspirations, Jessa?" He put his hand on the armrest of her chair and leaned forward. "Or were you hoping to talk about more personal matters?"

She wasn't getting anywhere. What if she just came out and asked?

"I'm wondering what you think about Will's variance for the amusement park. I'm surprised my dad never thought of it. He would have loved something like that next to the resort. It would have been great for business—for everyone in Timber Falls."

Beck pulled back. "Is that why you've come? Did Will send you?"

"No." Jessa shook her head. "He doesn't know I'm here. I was just curious what reservations you have. I was hoping I might answer any questions you have about how it would affect the resort or the town. I'm sure you want what's best for Timber Falls."

Beck studied her for a minute and then moved his hand to the back of her chair, a slow smile on his face. "Is that what you really want to talk about, Jessa? I remember the way we used to flirt in high school. You were interested—and don't tell me you weren't. I knew I would need to bide my time with you—and that time has come. We're both single. I could show you a good time."

The hair on the back of her neck rose and she pressed herself into the chair. "I just got out of a bad marriage and I'm trying to get my feet under me again." She put her hand on her stomach. "With the baby coming, I'm not looking for a good time. I'm looking for stability. A job. A permanent place to live."

"Is that all?" He leaned back a little. "I have a job right here in the office. I'm in need of another paralegal. If you're willing to work on certification, I can hire you immediately. It's a good, steady income and can provide well for you and your child. I can help you find a great place to live and even see that you have a little extra cash—on the side—for necessities. Consider it a *personal* loan."

Jessa's lips parted. She hadn't expected a job offer—especially from Beck Hanson. The job sounded ideal—something she would enjoy doing—if it was for anyone other than Beck.

The very thought of working for him every day made her stomach clench. Taking a personal loan from him would be disastrous. She didn't want to owe him anything.

"Thank you for the offer," she said as she started to rise out of her chair, hoping he'd back up. "But I have a lot to think about right now."

He stood but didn't give her the space she was hoping for, so she went around the other side of the chair.

"Why the rush to leave?" he asked.

"I should get back to the resort." She hadn't achieved her goal, so she decided to put in another plug for Will's amusement park idea. "If Will's idea is successful, which I know it will be, everyone will applaud you for helping him achieve it. If there's anything I can do to convince you to give him the variance, let me know."

"Well." He moved a little closer. "We can definitely talk about it. What do you say about going out with me tomorrow night? Supper, dancing—maybe a little moonlit stroll along the riverwalk?"

She maneuvered around him. "Maybe something a little less—date-like?"

"You don't want to go out on the town?"

"I'm pregnant, Beck. The last thing I'm interested in right now is a night on the town."

He glanced down, as if forgetting. "Maybe just dinner, then?"

"How about I come back here on Monday? I'll make an appointment with your assistant."

His lips thinned just enough for her to notice.

"If that's what it takes to get you to see me again," he said, "then I'll take it. But I plan to convince you to go out with me, Jessa Brooks."

She opened his door and stepped out into the hall. "And I plan to talk you into giving Will the variance."

He smiled. "Maybe we'll both have to compromise to get what we want."

Jessa studied his face, trying to decide if Beck Hanson was bluffing.

She wasn't sure.

Will stood inside the main cabin alternating his gaze to the river, where families were swimming and boating, and the clock above the sink, wondering what was taking Jessa so long.

He wasn't usually the type to worry, but he felt protective of her in a way that he'd never felt for anyone else. Maybe it was because she was pregnant, and he wanted her to be extra careful. Maybe it was because of her past in Paris and the thugs that had threatened her. Whatever it was, he couldn't stop thinking about her safety. He should have asked her how long her errands were supposed to last, so he could have known when to start expecting her back. It had been two hours since she'd left, and he couldn't imagine what might be taking her so long. Was she at the doctor? Running errands for the festival? She probably wasn't shopping since she didn't have much money to speak of.

She hadn't purchased much yesterday from his parents' store, though he suspected that she had more needs than she let on. He didn't know a thing about babies, but his cousin had a baby right after he moved back to Timber Falls and all the women in his family had given her a baby shower. He had helped her and her husband move everything into their house and he had been shocked at the amount of *stuff* needed for a baby.

Jessa had nothing for her baby. Would she need stuff, too?

But that led him to wonder where she would put her stuff.

He left the dining room and walked down the hall toward the bedrooms. The largest room was the one he had been occupying. The second largest was Jessa's bedroom—which he hadn't entered since she had come back.

But there was a third room. It wasn't very big and had been used for storage as long as he could remember. Jessa and her dad hadn't needed it as a bedroom—and Will hadn't, either. It was next to Jessa's bedroom and had a window facing the river.

Will entered it and turned on the light. Everything here had belonged to Oliver. Will hadn't gone through any of it. Maybe Jessa would want to see what it was and decide what to do with it.

And, maybe, if Jessa was planning to stay, they could turn it into the baby's room.

A noise in the living room made Will's pulse thrum. He hoped it was Jessa—not only because he was worried about her, but because there was an inexplicable feeling in his chest each time he was with her. It was warmth and happiness and pleasure, all wrapped up in a feeling he hadn't had in a long time.

"Jessa?" he asked as he left the room and turned off the light.

"It's me," she said. "Sorry I took so long."

He walked into the living room and noted that she looked a little more tired than usual. Concern filled him. "Everything okay?"

"Yeah—I guess."

He frowned. "Something wrong with the baby?"

She smiled and shook her head as she put her hand on her stomach. "No."

Relief washed over him, and he suddenly realized that the baby was becoming just as dear to him as Jessa. "Is it something else?"

She bit her lip for a second, as if she was contemplating what she would say.

"I had a few people to visit for the festival today," she said. "There are a couple of businesses that have agreed to be sponsors for the event and I wanted to introduce myself. It was silly of me to go on the Friday after the Fourth of July, since no one was at work. I'll have to go back Monday or Tuesday."

"I'm sorry. It probably feels like you wasted your time." Was that what had her looking so upset?

"Well—I did get to chat with a couple of people who are volunteering, so that's helpful." She stood behind her dad's old recliner, facing him. "But that's not all I did today. I wasn't sure I should tell you—but you'll probably find out anyway and I don't want you to be upset with me."

Will frowned. "What happened?"

"I went to Beck's office to talk to him about the variance."

Beck's name made Will's skin crawl. "From the tone of your voice and the look on your face I'm assuming it didn't go well."

"No. He kind of propositioned me—and I didn't like it. I thought I could be helpful, but I just feel—" She shuddered.

Will's senses went on alert. "Did he hurt you? Do something inappropriate?"

"No. Nothing like that—well, he was inappropriate, but nothing that I couldn't handle." Her lips came together in a look of defeat and regret. "I'm sorry I couldn't be helpful, Will. I thought I could convince him, but I don't think I can approach him again. I've spent several years of my life dealing with men like him and I'm not willing to do it again."

Will's chest tightened and he walked across the room to Jessa. "You don't need to fight this battle for me—especially at the risk of your own discomfort and safety. You and the baby mean more to me than any variance."

As he said the words, something passed between him and Jessa—something he couldn't take back.

Something he realized he didn't want to take back.

They did mean more to him than the variance.

Jessa's gaze softened. "Thanks, Will."

"Please don't put yourself into situations like that again, Jessa." He couldn't shake his worry for her. "I appreciate that you were trying to help—but Beck isn't the kind of guy who is going to give in easily, unless he gets what he wants in return."

She lowered her gaze and her cheeks bloomed with color.

"Is that it?" Anger burned in Will's stomach. "He wants you in exchange for the variance?"

Jessa nodded. "Something like that."

That protective urge came over Will again and he shook his head. "When Beck doesn't get what he wants, he resorts to bullying and belittling people. I won't let him get away with it—especially where you're concerned."

"I appreciate that." She lifted her chin. "But I can fight for myself."

He smiled. "I know you can."

She returned his smile.

"We don't need to talk about Beck today," he said, wanting to put her at ease. "I have everything ready to go fishing—but I want to run an idea by you first."

He motioned for her to follow him down the hallway. "I know that your plans are uncertain—but I want you to know that you're welcome to stay as long as you want or need. Which means your baby is welcome, too."

She followed him and frowned with curiosity.

Will opened the door to the extra bedroom and flipped on the light again. "What do you think about turning this into the baby's room?"

Jessa looked at him quickly. "That seems like a permanent decision."

"Not really. Even if you're here for another three months, you'll need somewhere to put the baby's *stuff*." He didn't know what else to call it.

"What about you? Will you stay out in the boathouse until we're gone? What if it's winter? The boathouse is no place to live in the winter."

"I can move into one of the cabins for the winter," he said. "They're rarely used, except around the Christmas holiday season, and I can figure something else out at that time, if need be."

Jessa's face filled with such a sweet look, it almost hurt Will to see it.

She reached out and placed her hand on his. "Thank you." She tried to smile, but it was a little wobbly. "You don't owe me anything, Will."

"I know."

"That's why it means so much to me that you'd make this offer."

He couldn't find the words to respond while her hand was on his, so he let the silence linger for a second before pulling away from her gentle touch and walked into the room. "All of this is your dad's. Feel free to go through it and figure out what you want to keep and what you want to throw or donate. I can borrow my dad's truck if we need to make a trip to the dump or to the thrift store to donate."

She didn't say anything, so he finally turned around and found she was wiping away tears.

Will's heart broke. It had broken before—had actually been shattered. But this was different. This time, instead of breaking because of Jessa—it broke with Jessa. It broke for her, for her baby and for what might have been.

"Thank you," she said, through her tears. "You don't know what it means to have a safe place to bring my baby home to. For a long time, I wasn't sure if I would have a home for him or her."

In that moment, as far as it depended on him, he decided he was going to give Jessa and her baby the life they deserved. Not because he owed it to her, but because he wanted her to have it.

Chapter Eight

The week slipped by quickly as Jessa worked at the resort, made plans for the festival and cleaned out the extra room in the main cabin. At first it was hard to go through her dad's old things. He had saved all her schoolwork and homemade gifts she had given him for Father's Day and his birthday. But, he had also saved family photo albums, old family letters and even her mother's diary. She had loved this peek into her family's past, especially her mother's private thoughts and experiences. Growing up, Jessa had felt close to her mom through her dad's stories and her grandparents' memories. But having her mother's writing was something else entirely.

Jessa took the diary to her room and read a few pages each night. The diary started when her mom was in college, around the time she met Jessa's dad. Flipping forward, Jessa saw that it ended soon after Jessa was born, and her mom became sick. Would there be anything within the book that might encourage and help Jessa in her own pregnancy? Part of her wanted to savor the diary as she read it for the first time. The other part wanted to rush ahead.

As she went through the storage room, Jessa had filled a box with items she planned to keep but found much more that she would throw out, like old newspapers, books and magazines, and things she would donate, like her dad's old clothes, unused household items and a couple of pieces of furniture they didn't need.

By the end of the week, the room was empty, the walls were repainted a light cream color and Will had steam-cleaned the carpet. It looked and smelled brand-new.

But it was still empty.

Jessa was contemplating this as she turned off the laptop in the lobby on Friday afternoon. All the new visitors had checked in and were settling into their cabins for the weekend or the week and Jessa was ready to head into Timber Falls for her first doctor's appointment.

Sandy had recommended a doctor that had come to town a few years ago and had delivered many of the babies at their church.

Jessa was a little nervous as she left the lobby in search of Will to tell him she was leaving. How would she explain to the doctor that she hadn't had any medical care for her and her baby? Would the doctor be upset at her? Make her feel guiltier than she already did? She would have seen the doctor sooner if there had been an opening, but today was the first appointment the clinic could offer her.

Will was entering the cabin through the back sliding door as Jessa walked into the living room from the lobby.

Their gazes met across the space, and she smiled.

Over the past week, they had found a gentle rhythm to their days. After the chaos and uncertainty of her life in Paris, the simplicity of the resort was refueling her soul and healing the broken pieces. Coffee on the deck at sunrise. Breakfast in the kitchen. Working around the resort. Lunch inside or out, depending on the weather. More chores or errands in the afternoon. And then supper together, followed by fishing, a walk, watching the sunset and then stargazing, a campfire or a movie.

Then, Will would say good-night and head to the boathouse and Jessa would return to her old room to reminisce about the life she had led—both in Timber Falls and beyond. But always, before her eyes slipped shut, and she fell asleep, Will was the last thing she thought about.

As he closed the sliding door, she was certain that William Madden was one of the most incredible men she'd ever known. She had suspected it for a long time—but now she was positive. He was a kind, hardworking, wise and faithful man of God.

"Hey," he said, his smile gentle and inviting. "Ready for your appointment?"

"I was just coming to tell you that I'm going to head there now."

Will hesitated—but then he walked toward her, meeting her in the living room.

"Can I come?"

His tender question caught her off guard.

"You want to come?"

"If you want me there." He studied her. "There are just some things we shouldn't have to do alone, if we don't want to. And going to the doctor is one of them."

Emotion welled up inside her and she nodded. "I am feeling a little nervous. I don't know what the doctor is going to say when she finds out I'm seven and a half months pregnant and haven't been examined yet."

"Don't worry about what she thinks," he said. "You're seeing her now and that's all that matters."

Jessa felt better knowing Will would be there to support her. It was yet another thing he didn't owe her—but she was starting to realize that Will's friendship wasn't out of obligation, but care and concern.

She grabbed her purse, and they locked up the cabin and went to his car.

The clinic had changed a lot since she was a kid. It now had a new second-floor addition and expanded wings.

Jessa stepped out of the car and glanced up at the sky. The day was cooler and overcast, but the forecast promised it wouldn't rain until later that evening. They had entered the heart of July and the weather could be unpredictable. Hot and humid one day, cool and raining the next—or picture-perfect.

They walked into the clinic together and Jessa checked in at the front desk, then they went to the waiting room.

There were several other people waiting. Moms and little kids, couples, elderly adults with caregivers and a few single people spread throughout the room.

Jessa didn't know any of them.

"Do you want me to wait out here for you?" Will asked.

"You don't want to come into the exam room?"

"If you want me there, I'll come. Are you sure it won't be a little—uncomfortable for you to have me there?"

She glanced at the door where the nurse would call them back. "I don't know. I've never had an appointment like this. I'm not sure what they'll do."

"How about I come with," he said, "and, if at any time, it gets uncomfortable for you, you can let me know."

She smiled at him. "The same goes for you. If you're uncomfortable, you can leave."

"It's a deal."

The door opened and a nurse appeared. "Jessa Brooks?"

"That's me," she said as she stood, mindful of her growing stomach. It was getting harder and harder to do simple things, like get in and out of a chair.

Will reached out and helped her.

They followed the nurse to a scale, and she took Jessa's

weight. She was happy to see she had put on a few more pounds since coming to Timber Falls. After that, they went into an exam room.

The nurse took her temperature, blood pressure and pulse, and then asked a few questions. When she was done, she said the doctor would be with them soon.

Jessa hadn't felt this nervous in a long time. She lifted her hands and noticed they were shaking—but then Will reached over and took one into his own.

She looked up at him and he smiled.

"You don't have anything to worry about, Jessa. I'm here. We'll figure all this out together."

Warmth and affection flooded her heart for Will.

"Thank you."

The door opened and the doctor entered. She had a pleasant smile and kind eyes.

Will let go of Jessa's hand.

"Hello," the doctor said. "I'm Taylor Smith. It's nice to meet you."

Dr. Smith shook Jessa's hand and then Will's.

"I'm Jessa and this is Will," Jessa said, her voice a little shaky.

"Dad?" Dr. Smith asked Will.

"No." Will shook his head. "Just a good friend."

"Just" a good friend didn't really sum up their relationship, but there was no way to explain.

Dr. Smith nodded, but didn't inquire further.

She sat down and faced Jessa, concern in her gaze. "I glanced at the notes on your chart and see that this is your first prenatal appointment."

"Yes," Jessa said quickly, explaining her situation in France. She didn't want to make excuses—but she needed to be honest, so she told her about the divorce and the lack of money to see a doctor there.

"I'm so very sorry for all that's happened," Dr. Smith said, her empathy making Jessa feel like she was in the right place. "Don't worry, though. Women have been having babies since the dawn of time, and though we have some wonderful technology and advancements to help in difficult situations, the majority of pregnancies need no intervention. Your body was designed to bring this baby into the world and if you haven't noticed any strange symptoms or have concerns, then I'm sure everything is just fine. But—" she paused and gave Jessa a serious look "—we won't know until we've done an exam and a few tests."

Jessa nodded. "Whatever we need to do, I'm ready."

"Good." Dr. Smith smiled. "First, let's get an ultrasound so we can check the baby's growth and heartbeat and then I'll do a physical exam. After that, we'll get some blood work and other samples and then we'll send you on your way. Does that sound okay?"

"It sounds great."

"Perfect. Let's head to the ultrasound room and have a look at your baby." She paused. "Do you want to know if it's a boy or a girl?"

Jessa glanced at Will. She hadn't even considered the possibility.

He smiled at her but offered her no indication as to his preference. It was up to her.

"It would be helpful in planning," Jessa said. "What do you think, Will?"

"Whatever you want, Jessa."

She nibbled her bottom lip. "I think I want to know."

"Perfect." Dr. Smith stood and opened the door. "Follow me."

They walked down the hallway to another room and Dr. Smith indicated that Jessa should lie on the exam table.

"Do you want me to leave?" Will asked Jessa.

She shook her head and reached for his hand. "No."

He gently squeezed her hand and stood next to her as Dr. Smith prepared her for the ultrasound.

Having Will's steady presence at her side filled Jessa with the confidence she needed to face this new experience. She rarely thought of Philippe, though so much of her life had been focused on him the past few years. Any time she thought about him it was with relief that he no longer had control over her life. But, in moments like this one, when he was not there to see his child, she grieved for what could have been—or should have been.

But God had brought Jessa back to Timber Falls and into Will's life, and she was discovering that she preferred what *was*. The truth was, she didn't want anyone else at her side right now.

Dr. Smith laid a paper blanket over Jessa's lap and then pushed her shirt up to reveal her rounded stomach.

Jessa glanced at Will and his gaze moved from her stomach to her face, wonder in his eyes. He smiled at her, and she returned the smile, so thankful for him.

"Are you okay being here?" she asked him.

"I honestly can't think of any other place I would rather be right now," he said with sincerity in his voice. "I've never been more certain that I'm in the right place—for the first time in my life."

She couldn't contain her grin. "Thank you, Will."

He squeezed her hand again as the doctor applied warm gel onto her stomach.

"Are you ready to see your baby for the first time?" Dr. Smith asked.

"I am."

The doctor laid the ultrasound probe onto Jessa's stomach and a black-and-white image showed up on the screen, immediately followed by a steady, whooshing heartbeat.

Jessa caught her breath as she saw the side profile of her baby. The little nose, the lips and the chin.

"There's your baby," Dr. Smith said with a smile.

The baby moved, flailing its arms, and the doctor had to move the probe to get a better look.

"Want to see it in 3D?" she asked.

"Yes." Jessa nodded, trying not to cry. She was looking at her baby. *Her* baby.

The doctor pressed a few buttons and the image on the screen turned to a peach color and Jessa saw her baby's sweet face in 3D.

A sound escaped Jessa—one of wonder and love.

Jessa felt the weight of Will's hand holding hers and she glanced up at him.

He was staring at the image of her baby, tears in his eyes.

And when he looked at Jessa, he grinned as he wiped away one of the tears. "It's beautiful," he said.

In that moment, Jessa Brooks was afraid she had lost the battle with her heart.

William Madden had held it years ago—and she was afraid she was letting it slip back into his hands once again.

Will couldn't explain the feeling that passed through him when he saw the baby on the ultrasound machine. It was both love and something else—something intense and stunning. The force of it brought tears to his eyes and he couldn't remember the last time he had cried.

It was probably the day he received Jessa's letter.

But these tears were different. This wasn't grief or

regret—the emotions that triggered these tears were from the very depths of love in his heart.

"Would you like to know the gender?" the doctor asked.

Jessa's gaze was locked on Will's, and he couldn't look away from her. He couldn't imagine what this moment felt like for her.

"Yes," Jessa finally said as she tore her gaze from Will and looked at the doctor.

"It's a girl," Dr. Smith said with a smile.

"A girl?" Jessa asked, just above a whisper.

"A girl," Will repeated, feeling just as protective of this baby as he did of Jessa.

Immediately, he could see this little girl running around the resort, finding toads and snails and dandelions like Jessa used to find when they were little. He could see her on the dock fishing and at the campfire, roasting marshmallows. He could see her smile and her wispy curls and hear the delight in her laughter.

But then he realized, with a start, that Jessa's little girl wouldn't grow up at the resort like Jessa had. If Jessa's plans succeeded, she would have a place of her own to raise her daughter.

A keen disappointment wrapped around Will, and he had to take a deep breath.

This wasn't his baby. This wasn't his life. He didn't belong here.

Yet—he wouldn't leave Jessa. Not now. And not until she asked him to.

"Congratulations," the doctor said a few minutes later after doing some measurements and checking several things on the ultrasound. "From all appearances, everything looks good. The baby appears healthy, and everything is progressing as it should. We'll just head back to the exam room and then get those samples and you'll be on your way."

"Thank you," Jessa said.

The doctor wiped the gel off Jessa's stomach and Will helped her to sit up.

"Are you okay waiting for me in the lobby?" Jessa asked.

"Of course." He helped her off the exam table and when they left the room she went right, and he went left.

He was happy to part ways with her for now. He needed some time to pull his emotions together and talk some sense into his heart.

"Will?"

He glanced up and saw Joy Asher in the waiting room. She and her husband, Chase, attended church with him, and she had graduated with Will and Jessa. They'd known each other most of their lives, though they hadn't been close in high school. Now, as Will had gotten to know Joy and her husband better, he considered them good friends. The Ashers lived in the Victorian mansion on the southern end of town that Chase's ancestor had built, and they operated a charity for widows and orphans in town. They also had three boys they had adopted, as well as their five-year-old twin girls, and another little guy, who was with Joy now.

"Hey, Joy," he said as he smiled at her and approached her in the waiting room.

"How's everything going?" Joy asked as she looked up at him. "I hope you're doing okay."

"Yeah—I'm not here for myself." He paused. He had taken Jessa to church last week and had introduced her to several people. Joy had been there, and they had chatted briefly, but she had to run to gather up her kids. Jessa mentioned that she had sat with Joy at the mothers of preschoolers gathering yesterday, too, so he knew that Joy was aware of the situation.

"Is Jessa here?" Joy asked, glancing around Will, as if she was waiting for Jessa to appear.

He nodded and took the seat next to Joy. "She just had her ultrasound and now they're doing an exam."

"I'm happy she was able to get in to see Dr. Smith. Everyone loves her and she's great at her job."

Will nodded, but he was still shaken by his emotions in the ultrasound room.

"Everything okay?" Joy asked as she handed her little boy a toy to play with as they waited.

"Yeah—everything's fine. I'm just—" He took a deep breath. "That ultrasound is pretty amazing."

Joy smiled. "I remember seeing each of my children for the first time on ultrasound. There's nothing that can prepare you for the emotions it triggers."

Will couldn't form the right words to agree with her.

"A few of us at the mothers of preschoolers group were talking," Joy said. "We'd like to host a baby shower for Jessa at my house, but we're hoping to surprise her. Do you think you can help us?"

"I'd love to." Relief filled Will. He was thankful the ladies at the church were going to step up and help Jessa. He felt helpless, not knowing what she needed.

"Great. If you can help us figure out what she needs—"

"Everything. She literally has nothing for the baby."

"Oh." Joy nodded, as if in thought. "I don't think we can help with everything she needs, but we can make a good dent."

"I'm clueless about all of it. Do you know what she'll need?"

"Yes—but I couldn't possibly give you a list right now.

I'm sure she has some thoughts." Joy's face lit up with an idea. "There's a flea market in Tanner's parking lot today and tomorrow. You should take her there. They always have gently used baby furniture at great prices. Even if she's not ready to make any purchases, it'll give her some ideas. And it's always fun to shop around. If she has some of the bigger items, we can focus on the smaller stuff like diapers, bottles, clothing, thermometers, all that stuff."

"That's a great idea." Will felt relief again. At least he knew how to proceed.

"Shepherd Asher?" a nurse said from the door, indicating Joy's toddler.

"I'll see you soon, Will," Joy said as she lifted her son and smiled. "Bye."

"Bye—and thanks. I'll be in touch."

"Great."

Joy followed the nurse, leaving Will alone again.

He waited for another twenty minutes before Jessa appeared. She was smiling.

Which made him smile. "Everything go well?"

"Perfectly. Dr. Smith said that all the preliminary tests look great, and she has no concerns."

"I'm happy to hear that, Jessa."

"Me, too. You have no idea how worried I was."

They walked out of the building and toward Will's car. "I have a surprise for you. Do you feel up to a little shopping?"

"Groceries?" she asked.

"No." He smiled and opened the passenger door for her.

She got into the car and frowned. "What kind of shopping?"

"You'll see." He drove her across town to the flea market.

"What is this?" Jessa asked as she looked out at all the

tents and vendors. There were dozens of people meandering through the secondhand items.

"It's a flea market. I ran into Joy Asher, and she mentioned that they usually have gently used baby furniture here, at affordable prices. I thought we'd take a look."

Jessa made no move to get out of the car. "I can't afford to buy furniture right now."

He took her hand and she turned to look at him. "I want to buy a few things for you, Jessa. Like a crib and a high chair. I'm sure there are other things you'll need, too."

"I can't ask you—"

"You're not. And please don't refuse me. You're working hard at the resort, and I'm not paying you what you deserve. Let me do this for you and the baby."

Jessa took a deep breath and then nodded. "Okay."

He smiled. "Good. Let's go."

They got out of the car and started looking at the items under the tents. Some of the vendors had baby items and some didn't. They asked around and learned that the vendor with the furniture was toward the back.

Once they arrived, Will was shocked at how many options they had.

As they started to compare items, it was clear Jessa had a preference, but the crib set she liked was a little more expensive than the others. It included a crib, a changing table, a dresser and a rocking chair.

"You should get it," Will said.

"It's too much."

"No." He shook his head. "It's not."

"I should just get the set with the crib and dresser. I can use the top of the dresser as a changing table."

"You want the dark one," he said to her, smiling and trying to cajole her. "You should get it."

"I can't."

"Okay—but I can." He walked up to the vendor and made an offer on the set. They haggled back and forth for a few minutes and finally agreed on a price. Will paid the man, who said his teenage son could deliver it immediately for free.

"I can't accept this gift," Jessa said as they walked away from the vendor. She put her hand on his arm to stop him.

Will turned to look at her—and without thinking, he laid his hand on her stomach. "It's not just for you," he said gently. "This is for her, too."

Jessa's gaze filled with warmth, and she pressed her lips together.

The baby rolled under Will's hand and his eyes opened wide. "Did you feel that?"

"I think she likes you," Jessa said with a laugh.

The baby rolled again, and Will took a step closer to Jessa, his heart beating hard. He'd never felt anything like it before.

"That's amazing," he whispered as he gazed into Jessa's eyes. "And to think you feel it all the time."

"It *is* amazing," she whispered back, color filling her cheeks.

"I think I would give this baby the world, if I could, Jessa. Please let me do this for you—for both of you."

She placed her hand over his and nodded. "Okay."

Will felt energized and excited—and he wasn't quite sure why.

Maybe Jessa and the baby wouldn't be with him forever—but they were with him now and he was going to enjoy every moment—no matter how much he might regret it.

Chapter Nine

J essa wanted to continue protesting, but she knew it wouldn't work. Will had decided to gift her and the baby— her daughter—with a bedroom set and she couldn't say no. Not that she wanted to say no, but it was getting harder and harder to take his charity. He tried to assure her it was his way of paying her for her help at the resort—but it still felt like charity sometimes. And since she wasn't in a position to say no, she decided to accept it with grace.

Someday, she would have her life figured out and pay Will back.

Not for the first time that week, she thought about Beck's offer to give her a job at his law office. She even went online and looked for information about paralegal responsibilities and what it would take to get certified. It sounded like something she could do and be good at, while enjoying the work.

If only Beck wasn't the one offering her the job. That was what she kept coming back to.

Beck Hanson.

She hadn't seen him since visiting his office, though Will had gone to a city council meeting on Monday night to petition for his variance to be put on the agenda. Beck had tabled the matter, once again, and Will had come home frustrated.

But as they pulled up to the resort, Jessa pushed it all aside for now. The flea market vendor had sent his son with the bedroom set and he was right behind them with his truck.

They would take the items into the cabin and Jessa would set up her baby's bedroom.

After they got out of the car, Will directed the teenager to park close to the main cabin and then he said to Jessa, "Let us know where you want things placed in the bedroom."

Jessa nodded and went inside to look at the space one more time. She'd already thought about where she might like the crib and the dresser, but now she would need to decide on a place for a changing table and the rocking chair, as well.

Will arrived in the room first with the rocking chair.

"I'd like that next to the window," Jessa said. It was easy to imagine rocking her baby and looking out at the river.

Will nodded and set the rocker where she pointed, then he left the room and was gone for a long time before he and the teenager came in with the dresser. Jessa had them set it against one wall, and when they brought in the changing table and then the crib, which would still need to be assembled, she had it all laid out. The room wasn't very big, but the furniture fit perfectly.

As Will was helping the teenager put all the ropes and moving blankets back into his truck, Jessa was left in the room alone. She went to the rocking chair and took a seat, swaying back and forth gently as she placed her hand on her stomach.

A girl.

She was going to have a baby girl.

There hadn't been a lot of time to soak in the news, but

now, as she sat in the baby's room—in Jessa's childhood home—she let the tears start to fall. If only her mom and dad could be there to meet her baby. At least they would be connected to her through this place—even if Jessa had to come back and visit it once she moved on.

A noise brought Jessa's head up and she found Will leaning against the doorframe, his hands in his pockets as he watched her. His blue eyes were so gentle, so calm and reassuring. She had the urge to wrap him in a hug—so she stood and walked across the room to do just that.

He seemed surprised, but soon enfolded her in his embrace.

She laid her cheek against his chest, mindful of the baby bump between them, and let out the most contented sigh she had uttered in years.

"Thank you," she whispered. "For everything. For taking me in, for showing me kindness, for being there with me today—and for offering me the gift of a home."

Will placed his hand on the back of Jessa's head and then kissed her forehead.

She closed her eyes, loving how it felt to be cared for and treasured again.

"I would do anything for you, Jessa," he said, his voice gruff and filled with emotion. "You know that, don't you?"

She nodded, unable to find her voice.

"You, your dad—and now your baby—you're like family to me."

Jessa's heart beat hard and she recalled Will's tears when he saw her baby for the first time during the ultrasound. He meant what he said—and it was so refreshing to know she could trust his words.

She pulled back and looked at him. They were so close. Her eyes drifted to his mouth, recalling all the kisses they had once shared. She became breathless as his lips parted. Was he thinking the same thing?

She was falling in love with William Madden all over again—but she knew it was a foolish notion. She looked down at his chest, trying not to think about kissing him. He deserved someone that was worthy of his love. Someone that could give him everything his heart desired—and not someone who was broken and needy. Ever since she had arrived, she had taken and taken and taken. He needed someone who had everything to give—and nothing to take.

Jessa pulled away completely, wiping her cheeks. "Thank you," she said.

He opened his mouth to respond, but the bell rang from the lobby and Will's shoulders sagged.

Jessa felt relieved. It was probably one of the renters needing something.

"I'll get it," she said. "Pull my weight around here." She tried to joke, but it sounded flat.

She left the baby's room and walked down the hall, through the living room, and entered the lobby, trying to shake off the thoughts and feelings she'd just had.

Beck Hanson stood there wearing a pair of navy blue shorts and a white button-down shirt, open at the neck. He was as relaxed as she had seen him since returning to Timber Falls. And he looked different somehow—contrite maybe?

"Hey, Jessa," he said.

She stood in the open doorway, not willing to enter the lobby with him. "Hey, Beck."

He let out a deep breath. "I know you're probably leery of me after what happened in my office last Friday. I felt foolish all week and it's taken me this long to get up the nerve to come here and face you. I want to apologize. I came on too strong, too soon, and there's no excuse for it. You took me off guard and my insecurities took over and I was foolish. Will you forgive me?"

Jessa lifted her eyebrows at his rapid confession. This didn't sound like the Beck Hanson she knew. He was usually loud and boisterous and rude.

"I know you have no reason to trust me," he said, taking a step closer to her. "But I really am sorry, and I'd like to make it up to you."

"That's not necessary, Beck." She shook her head. "I forgive you. You don't owe me anything."

He looked down at the sunglasses in his hands. "Okay—but I would like to talk to you about the variance. I've heard everything Madden has to say. I need some Brooks family perspective. After all, your family started this resort and the yearly festival. Both are part of the Timber Falls legacy and everyone in town has nothing but good things to say about your family. Maybe what the amusement park idea needs is the Brooks family stamp of approval."

Jessa's heart leaped at the thought. "You'll consider the variance for Will?"

"Maybe—but only after I've had a chance to hear your thoughts."

"I have so many of them." Jessa stepped into the lobby, eager to share her ideas. "This resort has been part of the fabric of this community for three generations and I want it to be here for the fourth. Times change and we need to meet those changes with innovation—"

"Whoa," Beck said, putting up his hands, chuckling. "I like the enthusiasm, but I don't have a lot of time right now. Let's plan to get together for a lunch meeting—say Monday afternoon? Pull your thoughts together and let's meet at Ruby's Bistro at noon. I can pick you up—"

"I can get there myself." Jessa still wasn't sure she could trust Beck. Her ex-husband had been a smooth talker when it benefited him. But when it didn't, he was a monster. She wasn't about to get into a car with Beck. "I'll see you at noon at Ruby's Bistro on Monday. And I'll be ready for the meeting."

"Great." Beck grinned. "I'm excited about what we can accomplish together, Jessa. With your enthusiasm and my vision, I think we can do good things."

Was he talking about the amusement park variance? Or something bigger and broader?

"I appreciate the opportunity to talk with you," Jessa said, trying to keep her voice to a neutral pitch. "I'll see you on Monday."

"I'm looking forward to it," Beck said. "See you then."

He left the lobby with a bit of a swagger—which was more like Beck than the humble, contrite version that had entered.

Jessa's heart filled with hope. If she could help get the variance for Will, she might feel like she deserved the charity he was offering her. She might have something to offer him, instead of taking all the time. It buoyed her spirits, and she inhaled a deep, cleansing breath. She had spent years feeling like a burden to Philippe and hated feeling like one to Will.

But she didn't want to get Will's hopes up. She would keep her meeting with Beck quiet for as long as she could. If Will knew she was meeting with him, he'd probably caution her not to—or do something to make Beck upset again.

When she reentered the baby's room, Will was kneeling next to the pieces of the crib, organizing them. He looked up at her, a question in his eyes.

"Someone need something?" Will asked.

She nodded, trying to be noncommittal in her response. It wasn't unusual for renters to come looking for a board game or a book to borrow from the resort's small library. "I took care of it."

"Good." He nodded at the crib, which had a mattress, but no bedding. "I was thinking you should make a list of all the things you might need, like blankets and stuff. We can see what we can find."

Jessa knew if she protested, he'd tell her he owed her, so she only nodded. She could make a list of needs—and at the top of the list would be the need to make sure Will had what he needed.

That was the most important thing to her.

The storm came in on a rolling cloud of thunder and lightning. The wind slashed the rain against the side of the house in wave after wave and Will was glad they were inside where it was warm and dry.

He'd kept busy putting the crib together and fixing up the set, trying to ignore whatever had happened between him and Jessa before the doorbell interrupted them. It had almost looked like she wanted to kiss him—but as the evening wore on, he wondered if he had imagined it.

"This storm isn't supposed to let up for a while," Jessa said as she looked at the forecast on her cell phone.

"We can always use the rain." Will slipped the drawer back into the dresser after reinforcing the bottom. The baby's bedroom set was secondhand, so it had been in need of some work. That was one of the reasons it had been cheaper than a new one, but Will wasn't opposed to the work. He enjoyed fixing broken things and bringing them back to life. "There," he said. "I think this drawer will hold up for at least twenty more years."

"Twenty years," Jessa said from her spot on the rocking chair where he had told her to rest after she had been busy washing the furniture. It had looked like it had sat in someone's garage or attic for a few years and had needed a good cleaning. "I can't even imagine twenty years from now. All of this will be in the distant past."

He glanced at her and found her rubbing her stomach. The memory of the baby rolling beneath his hands was fresh and powerful.

She was so pretty—even more beautiful with the glow of motherhood around her. Jessa would be an amazing mom. Will couldn't believe that Philippe had given it all up—and for what? What could possibly be more appealing than Jessa and their unborn child?

The thought stopped Will.

In his mind, there was nothing more appealing.

"Want to feel her again?" she asked as she looked up and caught him watching her. "She's really active right now."

Will wasn't sure. Part of him wanted to feel the baby again—to be near Jessa—but the other part knew he was getting dangerously close to losing his heart—especially after what had happened earlier. It was all too much. Being this close to her, experiencing all these moments of intimacy and wonder. The ultrasound, putting the baby's room together. These were things a couple did as they were expecting their first child. It was doing something to him that he liked—a lot—but shouldn't, because they *weren't* a couple, and this wasn't *their* baby.

Yet, how was he supposed to tell her no?

He set aside the wood glue he had been using and walked over to the chair. It was awkward to stand over her, so he got down on one knee next to the rocker.

Their gazes met and her dark brown eyes were so soft and gentle as she stared at him.

His breath caught as she reached for his hand and tenderly laid it over her stomach.

At first, the baby was still—but then it pushed against his hand and moved underneath his touch.

He grinned. "I never really thought about how it might feel to carry a baby inside you. Is it as weird as I think it would be?"

"Kind of," she said, moving his hand to follow the baby as it moved, "but you have plenty of time to get used to it."

"I don't think I'd ever get used to it." He studied her. "Are you afraid?"

"Of having the baby?"

"Of being a mom. Having the responsibility of a child."

"I'm scared that I won't be a good mom," she said, her voice low. "Especially because I didn't have a mom to raise me."

"Jessa." Will pulled his hand back and leaned his elbow on the armrest. "I don't know of anyone who is more suited to be a mom than you. You have everything a mom needs. You're kind, intelligent, thoughtful, caring and gentle. You are more than capable of being a *great* mom."

"You really believe that?" she asked.

"I do."

Thunder rumbled outside, drawing both of their gazes to the window.

"It's getting late," he said, conscious of the intimacy of this moment, too. "How about we go out to eat tonight? Treat ourselves after a long week."

"I have some ground beef thawing in the fridge," she said. "I don't mind whipping up a batch of spaghetti here. It's simple enough."

Memories of Jessa's spaghetti instantly made his mouth water. "I forgot about your spaghetti recipe."

"It's nothing special," she giggled. "Just a jar of store-bought marinara doctored up a bit."

"Whatever you do to it is amazing."

"I think your memory is faltering," she said. "There's nothing special about my spaghetti."

"Then maybe it's the good memories I have of sitting with you and your dad around the dining room table enjoying the meal with you that made it so special."

A sweet smile tilted Jessa's pretty mouth. "Sometimes, the people around the table make the meal better than any spice or ingredient you can add."

"Then it's going to be just as good as I remember," Will said, "because I'll be enjoying it with you again."

Her cheeks blossomed with color and pleasure filled Will. He loved making her blush and would try over and over again.

"I'll help," he said as he stood and offered her his hand. "Just tell me what I need to do."

They left the baby's bedroom and flipped off the light.

The rest of the cabin was dark and with the storm howling outside, it made the inside darker still.

On instinct, Will reached for Jessa's hand. The last thing they needed was for her to trip over something.

She grasped his hand and followed him into the kitchen.

Will's heart beat hard as he felt her soft skin against his. It was all he could think about as he reached for the kitchen light, wishing he didn't need to let her go.

"Wait," Jessa said, just loud enough for him to hear as she squeezed his hand.

"Wait?" he asked, turning to her.

"Let's watch the storm for a little bit." She motioned

to the sliding glass doors facing the river. Without the inside light reflecting off the glass, they would have a better view of the storm.

He continued to hold her hand as they maneuvered through the dining room to look at the storm—and he didn't let her hand go when they arrived at the window.

They stood for several moments—neither one speaking.

There was just enough light behind the clouds to offer them a view of the storm. Whitecaps foamed on the river and the trees bent under the force of the wind. Rain pummeled the door, the deck and the yard. No one was outside, and though the other cabins were full, Will felt like he and Jessa were all alone on the property.

Just the two of them and the growing affection in his heart.

If he wasn't careful, it would get out of control, and then where would he be?

Slowly, he let go of her hand and they stood side by side.

"We should probably feed that baby," he said, quietly. "You can stay to enjoy the storm and I can get it started."

"It's okay," she said, letting out a sigh.

What was that sigh about? Was she upset he had let her go? Upset that he had held her hand in the first place? Reluctant to step away from this moment? Frustrated that this moment had happened?

If they were in a relationship, he would have asked—but they weren't, and he couldn't even contemplate something like that.

He moved away from the doors and turned on the dining room light and then the connecting kitchen lights.

Jessa left the dining room and joined him in the kitchen without a word. She took out all the ingredients they would need for spaghetti, and he pulled out the pots and pans.

They worked in quiet companionship, but he wondered what she was thinking and feeling. Again, part of him wanted to ask—but the other part didn't want to open the discussion. They had no business talking about their feelings with one another.

For all intents and purposes, he was her boss. She was his employee. He needed to keep things professional at all times.

At least, that's what he kept telling himself.

Soon, the cabin was full of the smell of garlic, basil and oregano. Even though Jessa claimed there was nothing special about her doctored-up marinara sauce, he still watched to see what she added and found it wasn't a simple addition here and there. She had some precise measurements and a few ingredients he didn't expect, like red wine vinegar.

When his assistance was no longer needed, he sat on one of the stools and watched Jessa finish preparing the meal. She was focused as she cooked, and Will almost felt like he was intruding on her personal space. This kitchen belonged to Jessa. It had been hers growing up as she helped to care for her father, and it was hers again now.

She fit here. In this kitchen. In this cabin. At this resort. And in his heart, where she was settling in, whether he liked it or not.

What might it be like to do this with Jessa, day in and day out, for the rest of their lives? To continue in this happy, content pattern they had slipped into this past week? Could it always be this easy? This effortless? Or would it get complicated if they got their hearts involved? If he wasn't careful and fell for her like he had as a teenager? Would his heart be safe in her care?

As soon as those thoughts hit him, he was reminded of how it had all ended. How Jessa had left him with nothing but a cold letter and had gone off to give her heart to someone who didn't deserve it. A man who had left her and her baby in a desperate and dangerous situation. With the broken pieces of her life scattered.

The pieces that Will was now picking up and helping her put back together.

He wasn't resentful about helping her—on the contrary. He was thankful that God had put him in a place to be useful.

He was just angry that it had happened in the first place. That Jessa had given up what they had for a man who didn't deserve her love or devotion. And that anger boiled the longer he thought about it. When he felt this way, it was easy to remember why he was keeping Jessa at a distance. He couldn't risk heartbreak for a second time.

And that included heartbreak from losing her *and* the baby.

"Should we just dish up here and bring our plates to the table?" Jessa asked as she glanced at him.

He had to force his emotions to quiet and offered her a smile. She didn't deserve his anger for something Philippe had done, because at the end of the day, Jessa hadn't set herself up to be hurt. She had entered the relationship with hope and trust—and he couldn't fault her for that.

After all, it was what he had done when he entered a relationship with her.

But he wouldn't put himself in a position to be hurt, either. He'd eat a quick supper with Jessa and then head to the boathouse where he could sit in silence and talk his heart into obeying.

Chapter Ten

By Monday, Jessa couldn't shake the feeling that Will was avoiding her. Ever since their meal together on Friday evening, she had hardly seen him. He didn't show up for coffee at sunrise, he made an excuse about grabbing a quick sandwich for lunch before she could make something, and he hardly said a word to her as they ate their supper together on Saturday and Sunday evenings. They had gone to church together Sunday morning, but even that had been quiet.

As her meeting with Beck approached, Jessa felt strange and out of sorts. She had mentioned to Will that she needed the car and he had told her to feel free to use it. He hadn't asked any questions, for which she was thankful, but his lack of concern was strange.

What happened on Friday to cause this change?

She drove toward Ruby's Bistro on Monday trying to think through everything that had happened and all they had said to one another. She couldn't think of anything that would have upset him, unless he was unhappy that he had helped her make a room for the baby in the cabin. Maybe that was why he was treating her like an employee—and not a friend. Was he having regrets? Second thoughts?

Jessa's heart was heavy as she parked the car and walked into the restaurant.

Ruby's Bistro was in the heart of downtown Timber Falls, across the road from the movie theater and down the street from the Maddens' grocery store. She had pulled together some notes for the meeting but was distracted because of Will's behavior and her own insecurities.

Did Will not want her at the resort anymore?

"Jessa!" Beck stood from the table where he was sitting and motioned her over as soon as she entered the bistro.

It was an eclectic restaurant with a garden mural on one wall and relics from old businesses decorating the rest of the space. Jessa had enjoyed going there as a teenager with her dad, but it had been a special treat to go out to eat.

"Thanks for meeting with me," Beck said as he held out a chair for Jessa and then took his own across from her. He was wearing a suit and tie and had to hold his tie back as he took a seat.

"I appreciate that you're willing to listen to my ideas," she said, feeling a little underdressed in her simple shorts and blouse.

"Of course." He smiled. "Before we begin, though, I'd like to apologize again."

"No need. I've forgotten about it." At least—she was trying to forget about his behavior at his office.

"Great."

The waitress brought water and menus for them and said she'd come back for their orders soon.

Jessa quelled her nerves by looking over the menu, which had changed quite a bit since she'd been there last.

When she put the menu down, Beck was watching her. She gave him a questioning look.

"I already know what I want," he said, not dropping his gaze from her face.

For some reason, his comment made her feel like

squirming—though he quickly added, "The Reuben sandwich is my favorite—but no matter what you order, you'll like it, I'm sure."

After the waitress took their orders, Jessa pulled out her notebook, ready to talk about the resort.

"Before we get into the amusement park," Beck said, "I'd like to reiterate my job offer. I'm in need of an intelligent and hardworking paralegal. I think you'd make a great addition to my staff, and I am willing to offer top dollar to get you to agree. I'll pay for all the certification classes and offer you a sign-on bonus, as well. Good paralegals are hard to come by and I'm willing to do whatever it takes to ensure you're on board. Have you had time to think about my offer?"

Jessa hadn't been prepared for this question, though, in hindsight, she should have known it was coming. "Honestly, I haven't given it much thought," she said.

Beck smiled. "At least it's not a no."

"It's not a no—" She paused, unsure how to proceed. It was a great opportunity, one she needed to take seriously. She had a baby to consider, and she needed a way to provide for her. She couldn't rely on Will's charity forever. The resort was supposed to be a temporary solution to her permanent problem. But it was so familiar, so safe, she hadn't wanted to think beyond the resort.

"I don't want to pressure you," Beck said. "And I know the baby complicates matters. You'll need time off when it's born—"

"It's a girl," she said.

Beck nodded. "Nice. As I was saying, you'll need time off when *she's* born and I'm in a position to offer paid time off. You can rest assured that you'll be taken care of, Jessa. I'm very loyal to my employees. You can ask any of them.

I know what it takes to keep good employees on and I'm willing to go the extra mile to help."

Jessa looked down at the table and nibbled her bottom lip. "When do you need my final answer?"

"I'd like it now, if possible, but I don't want to pressure you. I'd rather wait a couple of weeks and get a yes than demand an answer now and get a no."

"I'll think about it," she promised. "And let you know as soon as I can."

He nodded. "Good. I can wait a little while, but I'll need the answer sooner rather than later. I want to hire someone as soon as I can, and there's the added issue of you needing time off after the baby is born, too. We'll need to start the certification process and that takes quite a while."

"I'll try to give you an answer soon. But I also have the festival to think about. I'm committed to that—"

"How about you give me your decision after the festival wraps up?"

"That's still two weeks away."

"I can wait two weeks. I'll get by. And to show you I'm a good sport, I'll do everything I can to help with Riverfest. Do you need more sponsors? Donations? Sign my law firm up as a top donor. I can ask around for support, too. I like to help those who help me."

It seemed too good to be true, but Jessa couldn't be picky. She would take the next two weeks to make her decision and figure out what she wanted to do with her life. If she could work with Beck in a purely professional capacity, perhaps it wouldn't be too hard. She would talk to Clarice and the other employees and see what it was like to work for him. Maybe he had matured, and she had simply caught him off guard when she showed up at his office, like he said.

"Can we talk about the variance now?" Jessa asked.

The waitress arrived with the iced tea that Jessa had ordered and the lemonade that Beck had ordered, interrupting her comment.

When she left, Beck turned his attention back to Jessa. "What were you saying?"

"The varian—"

"Mayor Hanson!" a man said as he entered Ruby's Bistro. "Just the man I wanted to talk to. Say, there's a house on the west side of town, a couple places down from mine, that hasn't mown their lawn in about four weeks. There's an ordinance for that, isn't there? They have to keep their lawn mowed."

"There is," Beck said. "Be sure to call city hall and give them the address. Someone will give the property owner a citation and if it's not taken care of in forty-eight hours, the city will mow the lawn and send them a bill."

"Good to know. Say, I also have a complaint about a dog barking at all hours of the night."

Jessa sat patiently as the citizen made his complaints. The list was long, and he wasn't finished by the time their lunches were placed in front of them. Jessa wished Beck would give the guy the hint that it wasn't okay to bother them, but he listened to each issue and let the man know that something would be done.

When he *finally* left, Jessa had already started to eat her lunch, since it was getting cold.

"Sorry about that," Beck said. "A public servant is always on call—especially the mayor."

"Do people bother you all the time?"

"Not all the time—but quite a bit. I rarely go into public without getting approached at least once. I'm happy you started to eat. I'd hate for you to starve while Mr. Sorenson aired his frustrations."

Jessa nodded, her estimation of Beck rising a little more. He truly did take his job as mayor seriously and that was good to know. Maybe it was an indication of how he treated his employees and clients, too.

"Now," Beck said as he smiled at her. "Let's talk about the variance."

"You need to eat your lunch," she said, nodding at his food.

"I can eat and listen. Tell me why you think Will should get the variance."

"First—" she decided to tread carefully "—may I ask why you keep tabling the issue?"

He took a deep breath. "An amusement park, especially in a mostly residential neighborhood, is a big risk. I'm not only thinking of Will and his needs, but the needs of his neighbors or future neighbors. I don't want the value of anyone's property to decrease and I don't want the extra traffic to cause accidents or injuries. There's also the added crime possibility to think of. Amusement parks attract teenagers and teenagers are statistically more likely to get into trouble. There's a lot to consider and I don't want to make the wrong choice, either way."

Jessa frowned. "So, it's not simply because you and Will are old rivals?"

Beck scoffed. "Old rivals? In what way?"

She was starting to get a little uncomfortable. She distinctly remembered the way Beck had treated Will in high school because of basketball—and because of her. Was Beck pretending none of that had happened to make himself look less petty? Was this part of his ruse to get her to trust him and come to work for him? Or was he being genuine? One of her biggest regrets was trusting Philippe when she should have been leery of him. He was a smooth talker and he convinced her that all her fears and reservations were her problem—not his.

Was Beck doing the same thing to her?

She sat up a little straighter, choosing to act and believe with caution. "What would it take for you to agree to the variance? A letter of support from the neighbors?"

"I already have that. Will spoke to all of them and none of them have any major concerns."

"Then what? What else can he do to convince you?"

Beck looked down at his plate and seemed to contemplate her question. When he finally glanced back at her, he said, "To be honest, I'm not sure. I don't want to regret supporting this variance, so I'm biding my time."

Jessa frowned. "You're hoping he's going to give up, aren't you? You want him to throw in the towel and leave Timber Falls, because you can't find a good reason to say no to him."

For the first time, Beck looked at Jessa as if he was truly seeing her, and she caught a glimpse of the truth in his eyes. He did want Will to fail and give up.

But Beck would never admit it.

"I want to be certain," he said. "Plain and simple."

"Will's not giving up," she told him. "He is loyal to the Brooks family—to my dad's memory and my family's legacy. He made a promise to my dad that he'd ensure the resort continues operating, but the only way to make a real profit is to expand. Please, Beck. I want this for Will—but I want it for my dad and my grandparents, too." She put her hand on her stomach. "And I want this for my daughter. I'm asking you to please consider the variance for the amusement park."

Beck leaned forward, his face serious. "I'll consider your request when you tell me if you'll come to work for me. Is that a deal?"

"What you mean to say is that if I come to work for you, you'll give Will the variance."

Beck lifted a shoulder but didn't deny or confirm her accusation.

Which meant that she had a very serious decision to make, and she only had two weeks to decide.

Could she work for Beck Hanson?

If it meant that Will got his variance, she already knew the answer, but she'd still wait to tell Beck what she had decided until absolutely necessary.

Perhaps something would change, and she wouldn't have to work for Beck.

It was a far-fetched wish, but it was a wish, nonetheless.

Will tried to distract himself by working around the resort. He mowed and trimmed the property, which took him a couple of hours. He sprayed off the deck on cabin one after someone had spilled something sticky and didn't bother to clean it up themselves. He fixed a hole a neighbor's dog had dug near one of the flower beds in front of cabin five. And he restacked the woodpile near cabin four since the renters there had been using it for a nightly campfire.

But no matter how much Will worked, he couldn't stop thinking about Jessa and the previous Friday night. His thoughts returned to her baby, to her in the kitchen, to the laughter they had shared putting the crib together and the gentleness in her touch as she laid his hand on her stomach—and the moment when she looked like she wanted to kiss him. But his thoughts didn't stop there. He thought about all the years he'd had a crush on her in middle school, then how his feelings had deepened in high school and how he had lost his heart to her completely between prom and the end of the summer. And he thought about the future. A lot. What it would look like when Jessa left the resort.

When she was in New York or in Europe, it had been easier to forget about her. To know that she was going to be in Timber Falls—that he would probably see her at church each week—it would be impossible to forget about his feelings for her.

Because despite his best efforts, despite trying to talk his heart into listening to him, Will was still in love with Jessa—and his love was deepening with each passing day.

He sprayed cleaner on the windows on cabin two and wiped them down with a squeegee, trying not to think about Jessa. Again.

But it was impossible. He had tried to keep distance between them over the weekend, but he knew he was only hurting and confusing her. He could see it in her gaze and in the slope of her shoulders. He couldn't keep it up forever without alienating her—and he didn't want that, either. But how was he supposed to talk to her about what was bothering him? He could never tell her that his feelings were deepening and that he was going to be miserable when she left. Not only because it wasn't fair to her, but because his head was smarter than his heart. Acknowledging his growing feelings wasn't a good idea. He would have to force himself to stick with plan A and harden his heart toward her.

It took another hour to finish the windows and Will's stomach was growling. He hadn't stopped for lunch—but it wouldn't have mattered if he had. Jessa had taken the car into town just before noon. He had watched her pull out of the resort, trying not to be concerned about her and the baby. She was a grown woman. She was more than capable of taking care of herself—and she wasn't his responsibility. The sooner he accepted that, the sooner he'd get over his feelings.

Glancing at his phone, he saw it was after two, and she hadn't returned. It was probably for the better. He needed to grab something for lunch, and it would be easier to do it without bumping into her in the cabin.

Will set the cleaner and squeegee on the back deck of the main cabin and entered through the sliding door. It was a hot day, and the sun was beating down on him. The air-conditioning was a nice relief from the heat. He went to the sink and washed his hands and was about to grab a loaf of bread to make a sandwich when he heard Jessa enter the living room.

With a groan, he quickly pulled out the lunch meat, sandwich spread, pickles, tomato and lettuce from the refrigerator. Maybe she wouldn't come into the kitchen until after he was done. He could work fast.

It wasn't that he didn't want to see her—the opposite was true. He ached to see her. But each time he saw her, it was getting harder and harder to imagine a day when she would leave.

"Hey," she said as she entered the kitchen, pausing at the sight of him.

He felt grumpy and out of sorts, but he couldn't be rude. "Hey."

She set her purse on the counter but didn't make a move to say anything.

All she did was watch him.

He felt a little unnerved as he continued to make his sandwich, but he wouldn't ask her what she wanted.

"Did I do something?" she asked, her voice quiet—tentative.

He paused, his hand over the lunch meat, but still didn't look up at her. "What do you mean?"

"You ignored me all weekend. You're ignoring me now. Did I do something to insult you or offend you?" She paused and then said, "Are you having second thoughts about letting me stay here?"

This time he did look at her—and he could see that she was hurt—by him—just as he had feared.

"I'm not having second thoughts, Jessa." He felt defeated and sorry for hurting her.

"Then what? Did I say something? Or do something?"

"No." He let out a sigh and wiped his hands on a dish towel. How was he supposed to communicate his feelings with her? "You've done nothing wrong. It's me. I'm just working through some things. It's not your fault and I'm sorry."

She studied him for a second and then started to play with the strap of her purse. "I'm sorry, too."

"For what? You haven't done anything, Jessa." He felt even worse. She shouldn't blame herself for his bad attitude.

"I've inconvenienced you and—and I think I know what I'm going to do about it."

"What do you mean?"

"Beck offered me a job as a paralegal in his office—and it sounds ideal—except that I'd have to work for Beck. But I think he's harmless, really. He's a big talker, but I can handle that."

Will was shaking his head even though she wasn't looking at him.

"He wants me to give him an answer after the festival in two weeks, so I won't commit right now—but I want you to know that I'm not going to be in your way for much longer."

"Jessa." He was still shaking his head as he approached her. "Please don't do anything rash. I'm sorry—I'm not upset that you're here." He briefly closed his eyes. What he was really upset about was her leaving, but he couldn't say that. Not now. Maybe not ever. "You're welcome to stay as long as you want. I know I can't give you the kind of income that Beck can, but you'll always have a home and food and whatever you need." Even as he said the words, he knew he couldn't give her what she needed. Not really. She needed independence and the freedom to buy her own car, to purchase the necessities without feeling like she was a burden to him. "I can try to figure out a wage—but—" He was helpless. Until he could make more money, his hands were tied.

"Let's not worry about it for now," she said as she finally looked up at him. "I have a couple weeks to figure things out, but I wanted you to know so that if you were having second thoughts, you'd know that I won't be here forever. The baby and I won't be your problem much longer."

"Jessa, you're not a problem." He wanted to reach out and take her into his arms, to convince her that he wanted her in his life—but she had pulled away from him the other night, suggesting that she didn't want it. Even if she did— he couldn't offer her what she truly needed.

If only he could get that variance. He could expand and—it was the same old story. Over and over again.

His hands were tied because of Beck—and now Beck was trying to take Jessa, too.

Jessa walked around Will and went to the counter where he had been making his sandwich. She'd made a few for him and knew how he liked them.

As he watched, she put the sandwich together, cutting it down the center, and put it on a plate. She pushed the plate across the counter toward him—but when he went to pick up the plate, she didn't let it go.

Instead, she met his gaze and said, "Don't run off, Will. Stay and enjoy your sandwich in your kitchen. This is your home. I'll leave."

She let go of the sandwich and picked up her purse, then left the room.

A couple of seconds later, he heard her bedroom door close.

Will bent down and rested his elbows on the counter. He placed his face in his hands and groaned again, his appetite gone.

This wasn't how he wanted things to go between him and Jessa. He didn't want to live like strangers—and though he knew they needed to behave like employee and employer, that was impossible, too. They could never be so impersonal. If they were in the same space, it was inevitable that they would be drawn to one another.

Will had never felt so confused. He was attracted to Jessa—yet he knew it was foolish to pursue her. He wanted her to stay—yet he knew it was best for her and the baby to leave. He was falling in love with her all over again—yet there was no hope for a future with her. His mom had warned him not to get involved—yet here he was.

Why couldn't life be simple?

And why did Beck Hanson have to offer Jessa a job that she'd be foolish not to accept?

Chapter Eleven

It had been a week since Jessa had confronted Will in the kitchen and told him that she was thinking about taking a job with Beck. Since then, they had found a quiet coexistence. Will joined her in the mornings for coffee again, they ate lunch and supper together, and discussed the daily needs of the resort, but they never sat together in the evenings or discussed anything personal. Jessa sensed Will was trying to keep his distance and maintain a semiprofessional relationship. Yet—he wouldn't tell her what had changed or why.

But as the days passed, Jessa longed for more from Will. It was difficult to be so close yet not have the liberty to share everything with him.

She was just cleaning up lunch on Saturday afternoon when Will entered the kitchen.

"Do you still need to run into town today?" he asked her.

"Yes. Joy Asher said she has a check from the Asher Foundation she'd like to give me for the festival and asked me to stop by around one."

"Mind if I drive you?" he asked. "I'd like to run a few errands myself."

"Of course not." Jessa relished the idea of spending time in Will's company. She missed their easy camaraderie. With just a week left before the festival and the deadline to give Beck an answer, she was running out of time to figure out a different plan.

More importantly, she was running out of time with Will.

"I'll take a quick shower and then we can leave," he said.

He'd been working outside all morning and looked like he could use a cool shower. The resort was full, as usual. The sun was merciless, and the humidity was high.

"Great," she said. "I'll just change and be waiting for you."

She had never been to the Ashers' mansion before, but she had seen it from the road and heard from everyone that it was an impressive home. Jessa knew it was silly, but she wanted to dress up a little to visit Joy—though Joy was as down-to-earth as they came.

After starting the dishwasher, Jessa went into her bedroom and found a sundress to wear for the afternoon. Her growing stomach was making it harder and harder to fit into her clothes. She only had a month left before her due date and wondered how the baby could grow any bigger. Thankfully, several of the ladies from the mothers of preschoolers group had given her maternity clothes they no longer needed, and she had added a few things to her wardrobe. The sundress she chose for today was a simple, pink dress that went down to her knees and had thin straps over her shoulders. She put on a pair of sandals and a dab of lipstick and grabbed a white cardigan.

When Will entered the living room a few minutes later, he paused to take in her appearance. She was thankful she had taken extra care, since the look on his face told her he liked what he saw.

"You look very pretty," he said to her.

"Thank you."

He looked nice, too, in a pair of khaki pants and a short-sleeve button-down shirt. His blue shirt made his eyes shine and when he smiled, her legs felt a little wobbly.

They left the cabin and drove toward town.

Jessa wanted to say something—anything—that would ease this tension between them. But all she could think about was the impending decision she needed to make.

"Riverfest is a week away," she said.

"How are you feeling about everything?"

"Good. The festival committee has almost everything under control. I just need to get a few more donations and make a couple more decisions."

"I'm happy it worked for you to be involved. I know how much it means to you."

Jessa swallowed the nerves bubbling up inside her. "Beck will want an answer from me next week."

"I've thought about little else."

She glanced at him. "You've been thinking about me?"

He didn't look at her, but she could see the struggle in him. "I think about you all the time, Jessa. I've been trying to come up with a way for you to stay at the resort, so you don't have to work for him. But I can't think of any way that makes sense. Beck can afford to hire you—and I can't give you more than what I've already offered. If that's not enough—and I know it's not—then you need to do what's best for you and the baby."

She put her hand on her stomach and the baby pushed back. Jessa wanted to reach for Will's hand to feel, but she didn't dare. The last time was just before he had pulled back from her.

"If I didn't have to," she said, quietly, "I wouldn't."

They didn't speak for the rest of the drive and when they

pulled into the Ashers' property, Jessa was too overcome by the home to say anything.

The estate was spectacular, with a tennis court, enclosed pool and a white Victorian mansion. Just behind, the Mississippi River meandered along the property, sparkling in summer brilliance.

"Wow," Jessa finally managed to say. "I can't imagine living here."

"The Asher family almost lost the house," Will said. "Most of them live in Washington State now, which is where Chase Asher grew up. He used to come here for the summers to spend time with his great-uncle. That's how he met Joy. She was hired to do some light cleaning. Apparently, they fell in love, but when Chase's dad heard about it, he took Chase away and sent him to Europe. What he didn't know was that Joy was expecting twins, so four years later, when Chase came back to sell the mansion after his uncle died, he was surprised to find Joy living here with their daughters and her three foster sons."

"That's incredible," Jessa said. "And they were married and chose to stay here?"

Will nodded. "The extended family decided to start a charitable nonprofit organization for the town, since Timber Falls helped them establish their multimillion-dollar company. And Chase and Joy are the directors of the organization. They do a lot of good for Timber Falls."

A couple of dozen cars were lined up on the circular driveway in front of the historic mansion and Jessa frowned. "What are all these cars doing here?"

Will shrugged but didn't hazard a guess.

He parked his car and Jessa climbed out, looking up at the three-story mansion. It was beautiful with wavy-glass windows and dormers.

Will joined her and they walked along the driveway to the front door, where he rang the bell.

"Joy told me to be here around one," Jessa said. "But I feel like we're intruding on a party or something. Maybe she forgot she asked me to come, and she has something else going on."

"I'm sure she'll explain," he said as the door opened, and Joy appeared.

"You made it!" she said with a grin and a big hug. "Welcome."

Jessa received the hug, but she was a little confused. Joy was dressed in a pretty floral sundress and looked like she was entertaining guests. Jessa could hear them chatting in the foyer behind Joy.

"I'm sorry if I got the day and time wrong," Jessa said. "It looks like you're busy, so I won't bother—"

"Surprise!" Joy said with a gentle laugh. "Come on in. Everyone's here for you."

Jessa's mouth slipped open, and she looked to Will. "Everyone's here for me?"

Will was grinning from ear to ear.

"What is this?" Jessa asked him as she started to follow Joy into her home.

"A surprise baby shower from the church ladies and the mothers of preschoolers group," he said.

"And you knew?" she asked, her voice betraying her shock.

"Of course. I was supposed to get you here at exactly one ten."

"Will!" Jessa couldn't contain her joy as she turned and was greeted by several ladies she had met at the church. Each one was so excited to see her. They commented on her pretty dress and on all the fun things they had planned for the shower.

The mothers of preschoolers moms were there, too. She recognized Kate Dawson, the pastor's wife, as well as Piper Evans, Liv Harris, Adley Marshall and others.

Jessa greeted all of them, overwhelmed in the best possible way. These ladies had only known her for a couple of weeks, and they were throwing her a baby shower? Tears sprang to her eyes, and she had to force herself not to cry. She met Will's gaze, and his smile was so tender, she got choked up all over again.

"Come into the music room," Joy said a few minutes later to everyone assembled in the foyer and front parlor. "Will—that means you, too."

"I shouldn't stay," Will said as he started to back toward the door.

"Nonsense," Mrs. Caruthers said as she linked arms with Will. "We want you to stay."

He tried making a fuss, but none of them would have it. Mrs. Caruthers practically pulled him into the large music room where all the furniture had been moved to make a large circle.

The room was gorgeous—more like a cozy ballroom or a very large parlor. A grand piano stood in one corner, which was probably why it was called the music room. Floor-to-ceiling windows all around the room let in glorious sunshine, but window air-conditioning units cooled the room to a comfortable level.

"Here's where you'll sit," Joy said to Jessa. "First, we have some fun games to play to get to know you a little better, then we'll break for refreshments, and after that, the gifts."

Will looked horribly uncomfortable. He was the only man present—and he was given the chair next to Jessa. A chair that she had a feeling was usually reserved for the baby's father.

"I'm sorry," Jessa whispered to him as the ladies were taking their seats.

His smile was warm as he shook his head. "It's okay— as long as you're okay with me being here."

"Of course I am. I just don't want you to be uncomfortable."

He looked around the room and laughed. "I'm the only man in a room of about thirty ladies—including some very busy church ladies—so no matter what we're doing here, I'd be uncomfortable."

Jessa returned his laugh, feeling lighter and happier than she had in a long time. Not only because she and her daughter were being showered with love and gifts, but because this was the first time in a week that she and Will had laughed together.

The afternoon went by in a blur of fun and surprises. Jessa had never felt more loved or cared for than she did in that moment. And when she found out that Will had worked with Joy to create a list of things she needed, her heart expanded in ways she couldn't explain.

Sandy was there and Jessa discovered that she was co-hosting the shower. Whenever she caught Jessa's eye, she offered Jessa a sweet smile—one that told Jessa she was loved. Cherished. Accepted.

And that, more than anything, made Jessa want to cry.

Will loved watching Jessa glow. He had never been prouder of Timber Falls or his church family than he was today. Most of these ladies hardly knew Jessa, but they had rallied around her and treated her with the love and thoughtfulness they would give a lifelong friend.

At first, he had wanted to leave, but as he sat through the baby shower and had the opportunity to experience this with Jessa, he was thankful he had stayed. Just seeing her smile was enough of a reward. And he had learned a few new things about her while they played games. For instance, he learned that she had been named after her mother's father, who was named Jesse, and her mother's mother, who was named Tessa.

The more he discovered about her, the more he liked.

"I might have to bring back a truck and trailer," Will laughed a couple of hours later as he and a few of the ladies loaded his car with the gifts Jessa had received.

"Whatever you can't fit," Joy said, "I'll have Chase run over later."

They worked hard but were able to get all of it in the back seat and in his trunk.

Jessa hugged Joy and Sandy and a few of the other ladies and then got into the front seat. A couple of gifts were placed on her lap—things that wouldn't fit into the back— and then they were off again.

She let out a long, happy breath. "Wow."

He grinned at her. "Surprised?"

"I'm still so surprised," she said as she looked at him. "And you knew about this the whole time?"

"Pretty much from the very beginning. But I didn't want to spoil the surprise."

"Thank you, Will." She smiled at him. "For everything. This means a lot to me."

"You're welcome."

She talked all the way back to the resort, reliving moments of the shower that had meant the most to her. The food had been scrumptious, the games were unique and fun, and the gifts—all the gifts—were remarkable.

But as they pulled up to the resort, Jessa got quiet.

Will turned off the car and glanced at her.

She had a strange look on her face.

"Something wrong?" he asked.

"It's just—I was thinking about how I would set up the nursery with all these things, but it would be a waste of time. No doubt I'll be moving before the baby comes. It will make more sense to just store it in the extra bedroom for now—until I know where I'll be living."

Her words felt like a splash of cold water—because he, too, had been thinking about Jessa filling the baby's room with all these gifts.

"Even if you take the job with Beck," he said, quietly, "do you think you'll be out of here within the month? You're due in four weeks, right? You don't need to leave right away."

"I am due in four weeks, but the baby could come sooner or later." She paused and shook her head. "I hate feeling so unsettled, especially now, when I want to set everything up and prepare for my daughter."

"I'm sorry, Jessa." He let out a frustrated sigh. "I wish things could be different."

Neither one spoke for a couple of seconds and then Jessa sighed. "I suppose we should haul this stuff in."

Will didn't know what to say, so he simply opened his car door and started to move the gifts from the car to the cabin.

The first load he took in included a large gift bag of diapers. He stood in the baby's bedroom—or, more appropriately, the extra room—and stared at the furniture they had assembled last weekend. He couldn't shake the images he had already started to picture. Jessa, sitting in the rocking chair with the baby, singing a lullaby. Then, putting the baby to bed after a bath, in cuddly little pajamas. Reading books to her, playing with her toys—all things he had no right to envision.

Yet, he couldn't deny what his heart wanted.

He wanted Jessa and the baby to stay.

"You can put the bag in the crib," Jessa said as she walked into the room, interrupting his thoughts. "That's probably the best place to store it for now."

He turned, wanting to tell her that she should stay, but the doorbell from the front lobby rang, cutting off his thoughts.

It was probably for the best. What kind of a life could she have with him?

"I'll get it," he mumbled as he set the bag in the crib and left the room.

Why was he feeling so crabby all the time? Maybe he needed to go for a swim later. Burn off some of the angst he was feeling.

Try to get Jessa out of his head.

Will entered the lobby and wished he hadn't.

Beck was standing there in casual clothes—a grin on his face. "I'm here for Jessa," he said.

It took all of Will's strength to not lash out at Beck. By all accounts, Beck was the sole reason Will couldn't keep Jessa at the resort. If Beck hadn't offered a job to Jessa, she would be happy to stay.

Yet—could he ever pay Jessa what she was worth?

Will was in no place to stand in Jessa's way, so he mumbled something to Beck and then returned to the cabin—but Jessa was on her way out and they almost collided in the living room.

"Everything okay?" she asked him.

"Beck's here." It was all he could manage to say.

Jessa frowned. "What does he want?"

Will didn't want to find out, so he started walking toward the kitchen, but Jessa's voice stopped him.

"Stay with me?" she asked.

His heart clenched at those three simple words.

Stay with me.

Will nodded and followed her into the lobby. If she wanted him there, he would stay there.

Beck seemed surprised to see him again—but he forged ahead. "Hey, Jessa."

"Hi, Beck."

"I—ah—I came to share something with you."

"Oh?" She frowned.

Beck looked at Will. "Does he have to be here?"

Jessa also looked at Will and she nodded. "Yes."

Beck scowled, but forced himself to smile when he turned back to Jessa.

"I found a fantastic condo for you. It's near the river. Two bedrooms. Close to Maple Island Park. There's a little lawn for the baby. It's perfect—and with the salary you'll earn from working for me, it's affordable."

Jessa started to protest. "Oh, Beck—"

"Don't say no until you've seen it," he said. "I got an inside scoop on it, but as soon as it hits the market, it'll be gone in hours. We need to go now if we want to walk through it."

"I don't know— Will and I—"

"If it means that much to you," Beck said, rolling his eyes, "Madden can come."

Jessa looked at Will, and he could see that she wanted to tour the condo. It did sound ideal and if Beck promised she could afford it, then she needed to at least look.

"It sounds too good to pass up," Will said to her.

Disappointment flitted through her gaze—but he didn't

understand it. Why would she be disappointed in finding
a great house?

"My Porsche is waiting," Beck said as he motioned for
them to follow.

Will locked up the cabin as Beck helped Jessa into the
front seat. Will got into the back, right behind Jessa, and
felt like a third wheel in the cramped space. How could
he compete with Beck Hanson? In high school, Will had
trained harder, practiced more and studied basketball to
earn his place in the starting lineup.

Now, with Beck as mayor and a wealthy lawyer, there
was no way Will could compete.

It made him feel crabby again.

They returned to Timber Falls and Beck pulled into a
neighborhood near the river and the park, just like he said.
There were several rows of condominiums, two stories
high. Each had its own garage and small front and back
yards. There was a covered porch on the one that Beck
pulled into. Everything looked well maintained and safe—
which reassured Will.

"Here it is," Beck said to Jessa. "It belongs to a friend
of a friend who is planning to sell. I told him I knew of
someone who was looking for a place. I was able to nego-
tiate a great price. Of course, I'm sure that getting a loan
right now would be a hardship for you, so I'm willing to
finance it." He smiled at her, a gleam in his eyes. "We can
work out a repayment plan."

Will didn't like the sound of that.

"It's way more than I could ask for," Jessa said as she
shook her head. "I don't even know if I want to go in and
get my hopes up."

"Get your hopes up, Jessa," Beck said. "Every day, all
day, because good things are coming your way. I promise."

Will wanted to make Jessa the same promise, but he couldn't, so he sat in the back seat and fumed.

Jessa finally got out of the car and Beck walked her up the short sidewalk to the front door.

The owner was expecting them, so he let them into the condo.

Will followed.

He watched Jessa's eyes light up as she took in the well-decorated house.

There was a front living room and a connecting dining room with a kitchen in the back. Beautiful views of the river made the house feel cozy and familiar. The proximity to the park was another great feature.

Upstairs, there were two bedrooms and a shared bathroom. It wasn't a huge house, but perfect for Jessa and a baby.

Will stood back, silently, and watched as Jessa asked several questions. It was clear she was interested, and with each question she asked, Will felt a little more of their time slipping away.

Yet—Jessa deserved this home, and the life Beck was offering. He pictured her scared and unhappy in Paris, only dreaming of the opportunity to live in a safe home with the comforts of a loving community around her. Will couldn't think of any reason she shouldn't take the condo, except that he didn't want her to go.

He loved her. Loved the baby. Loved the idea of the life he wanted to live with her. He'd always loved Jessa Brooks, but this time it was different. He was smarter, less dreamy-eyed and naive. He knew the risks—but he also knew the rewards.

Yet, he wasn't free to tell her. She needed to decide what kind of life she wanted for her and her baby, without him interfering like Beck was doing.

Even if he told her he loved her, he didn't know how she would respond. Their relationship was tenuous and fragile. Would he ruin a budding friendship by telling her his feelings were running deeper?

Finally, it was time to head back to the resort.

Will stewed in the back seat as Jessa and Beck talked about the condo. Jessa's excitement was palpable, and Will understood why—he just couldn't get excited for her.

And he couldn't help feeling like Beck Hanson was winning.

Chapter Twelve

When they pulled up to the resort, Jessa's head was spinning with all the things that had happened that day. Between the surprise from the baby shower and the amazing condo that Beck had found for her, she felt like she was living someone else's life. It was all moving so quickly, she felt like she needed to play catch-up.

"Can you give us a minute, Madden?" Beck asked as he parked his car outside the main cabin. "I'd like to talk to Jessa privately."

Will didn't even bother to answer but got out of the back and strode into the house.

"What's his deal?" Beck asked, though Jessa suspected that he knew.

More than anything, Jessa wanted to talk to Will. Things had been strained between them, but he was a good and trusted friend. She wanted his perspective to make her decisions.

As a light turned on in the cabin, Jessa became determined that she was going to confront Will and ask him what was bothering him. She needed wise counsel, and he was one of the wisest people she knew.

"I said I wasn't going to pressure you," Beck said to Jessa, "but time is of the essence where the condo is concerned.

The owner wants to get it on the market tomorrow—but if you haven't decided what you're going to do, I don't want to step in and make an offer on your behalf. I kind of need to know now."

Jessa's pulse thrummed. "I'm not ready to give you an answer now."

"What's going to change in a week?" he asked, his voice filling with impatience. "You have all the information you need to make your decision."

Jessa's gaze returned to the cabin—she couldn't help it.

Beck paused and looked in the same direction. "Unless you're waiting on Madden to make a move? Is that it? You want him to ask you to stay?"

Jessa's cheeks grew warm, and she couldn't look at Beck. She didn't want him to see the truth.

"He's in no position to make you an offer, unless his business picks up," Beck said. "And his business won't pick up until he has the amusement park. And, he can't build the amusement park until—"

"You give him the variance," she interrupted. "And you won't give him the variance unless I agree to work for you."

"Exactly." Beck smiled. "That about sums it up."

Jessa nibbled her bottom lip as she contemplated her options. Even if she took the job with Beck and moved out of the resort, that didn't mean she wouldn't see Will anymore. It wasn't like she would be forced to leave Timber Falls.

Granted, it wouldn't be the same—but maybe their friendship needed some distance.

She'd miss the resort, but she could visit whenever she wanted. However, it might be awkward to return, especially with the way things had been going.

Her other concern was that Will needed her help. Ever since she'd arrived, he had been free to keep up with the maintenance of the resort. But once he had the variance, he could add on and afford to hire someone else.

Going to work for Beck was the best option—for all of them.

Jessa took a deep breath and nodded. "If you promise me you'll give Will the variance," she said, "I'll work for you."

A grin broke out on Beck's face, and he fist-pumped the air. "Yes! You won't regret it. You're going to have the life you've always dreamed of."

Jessa's gaze returned to the cabin, her heart telling her the life she dreamed of was right here.

"Promise me," Jessa said to Beck. "I need to hear you say you will give Will the variance."

"I promise," he said.

"Okay." She had hoped to feel like a weight had been lifted from her shoulders, but she had never felt more uncertain in her life.

"I'll let the owner know we'll take the condo," Beck continued.

"*I'll* take the condo—not *we*." Jessa wanted to be very clear with Beck about where he stood.

"*You'll* take the condo," Beck said, "but I'll be the one financing it." He winked at Jessa. "You know, you're going to need to learn how to trust me."

Trust. What a strange word. Jessa had lost trust in almost everyone and everything while she'd been married to Philippe. Was there anyone she still trusted?

Her gaze went to the cabin again.

She trusted Will.

"I'll call you later," Beck said, "to work out the details of our financial contract."

Jessa opened the car door, wishing she had a lawyer— one who wasn't Beck—to look over any contract he made.

"Bye," Jessa said as she got out of the car and walked toward the cabin.

Doubt plagued her. Had she done the right thing? Could she trust Beck? What if his contract put her in a position she couldn't get out of? Visions of men coming to her door to threaten her brought on panic and she put her hand on her stomach. She would have her daughter to care for now—was she doing the right thing?

Yet—if this meant Will could get the variance, there was no question.

She entered the cabin through the front lobby.

The house was quiet. Had Will gone to the boathouse?

As she walked into the living room, she couldn't see him there, either.

Where was he?

Jessa walked to the baby's room and stood at the open door for a few minutes. Would she be able to move into the condo in time to set up her baby's room? The owner said he wanted to move as soon as possible—but could he be out in a month? What if the baby came before that?

And what about furniture? The condo wouldn't be furnished. She'd have to find a bed for herself and furniture for the living room and dining room. She'd have to stock a kitchen, too.

Not only would it be expensive, but it would be time-consuming, and she was already so tired. Furnishing a house was the last thing she wanted to do in the final weeks of pregnancy and the first weeks of having a newborn.

Thanks to her church and mothers group, she had almost everything she'd need for her baby. That was a start.

She still couldn't hear Will in the house, and it made her feel lonely. She walked down the hall to her room and picked up her mom's diary. She'd read all the way through it and had her mom's perspective on early marriage, pregnancy and the birth of her child.

Jessa sat on the end of her bed and opened the book to the last page, written a week after Jessa had been born. Her eyes fell on the passage that hit closest to home.

In one short week, I've fallen in love with Jessa in ways I never thought possible. For twenty-four years I got along just fine—but now I can't imagine life without her. This feeling I have is so powerful, it's consuming and makes me both hopeful and terrified at the same time. What if I fail her? What if I can't be the mother she needs me to be?

There is one thing I know without a doubt, I would do anything in my power to protect Jessa and give her the life she deserves. There is nothing I wouldn't sacrifice for her, and no matter how much I might mess up, I want her to always know that I love her more than life itself.

And those were her mother's final words on paper.

Jessa closed the book and held it against her chest. Going to work for Beck was the sacrifice she would make for her baby. And knowing that her mother would understand helped Jessa to feel hopeful that she was making the right choice.

If she could have her heart's desire, she would stay at the resort and raise her daughter there. But she couldn't continue with Will the way things were going. And, if she stayed, he'd never get the variance. There was really no other option.

Except—her heart told her there was another option, one that would require the most sacrifice of all.

She put the diary on the bed and left the room.

Will was sitting on the back deck and the moment she saw him through the sliding glass doors, her heart confirmed what it wanted more than anything.

It wanted William Madden.

All she could see was his side profile as he looked out at the river. The sun was low in the sky and there were still boats in the water. But she could see that his gaze was further adrift, and his thoughts were not on the boaters.

What would it take for Will to ask her to stay—forever? Could he ever love her again—or had she ruined it forever? She regretted her eighteen-year-old self and the foolish decisions she had made. Why did her twenty-eight-year-old self now have to suffer the consequences? It didn't seem fair. She'd been an immature child. Starry-eyed and naive.

No matter what, she needed to talk to him. To tell him what she'd decided. She couldn't make Will love her again—but she could do this sacrificial act for his benefit and maybe he'd know how she felt.

Jessa opened the sliding door and Will looked up, questions in his beautiful blue eyes.

He appeared defeated and sad. Was she the cause?

"Beck left?" he asked.

Nodding, she took a seat next to him. "A while ago. I was just in my room looking at my mom's old diary."

"You found your mom's diary?"

She nodded again. "It's the only link I have to her—and it's beautiful. I'm so happy I found it."

"So am I."

They were both quiet again as Jessa began to rock. She laid her hand on her stomach, wishing there was a way to make the conversation with Will easier.

Maybe it would be best to just be frank.

"I told Beck I'd accept his job offer."

He looked out at the river and nodded. "It would be foolish not to."

"He made a promise to me," she said. "If I said yes, he'd give you the variance."

Will stopped rocking and turned his gaze toward her, frowning. "What?"

"That's why I agreed to do it. He promised he'd—"

"You didn't need to say yes to him for my sake."

Jessa also stopped rocking. "How else will you get what you want?"

"What I want?" he asked, shaking his head. "What I want is for you to live the life *you* want. Not for me, not for Beck, but for you. He's manipulating you and you fell for it."

Her heart rate accelerated. "I did it for you, Will."

"I didn't ask you to do it for me."

Tears came to her eyes, and she stood. "How can you be angry at me for helping you? For saying yes to Beck so you'd have what you want?"

He saw her tears and he stood, worry on his face. "I'm sorry, Jessa. Please don't cry." He ran his hand through his hair and turned away from her for a second. "It's just that it's *Beck*."

She wiped at the tears as they fell and he turned back to her, remorse in his gaze.

"I'm sorry." He used his thumb to wipe away a tear, his voice lowering. "I just don't want to see you get hurt again."

His skin felt warm against her and feather soft. Jessa's breathing became shallow as she realized how close he stood. Memories of being in his arms, of feeling his lips against hers, brought heat to her cheeks.

He watched her, his own emotions playing behind his gaze. Did he remember, too?

Will hated seeing Jessa cry, but when he knew it was his fault, he hated it more than ever.

Slowly, he lowered his hand away from her cheek, his pulse thrumming. It had been so long since he'd held Jessa—felt her in his arms. For months after she had left him, he'd lain awake at night, remembering the sweet moments they had shared. The first time he held her hand, their first kiss, the first time he'd told her he loved her.

All of it came rushing back to him now and he felt overwhelmed by the memories.

He took a step back, afraid he'd embarrass her.

"I'm sorry for reacting the way I did," he managed to say. "I've never liked Beck, but I think he wants to help you. I just wished you had made the decision for your benefit and not mine."

He couldn't live with himself if things went wrong for Jessa, and he was to blame.

"I didn't do it just for you," she said. "I did it for the baby, too."

"I know." He nodded and put his hands in his pockets so he wouldn't be tempted to touch her cheek again.

"I wanted to talk to you about it," Jessa said, "but you've been so distant this past week."

"I'm sorry, Jessa." He shook his head. "You deserve so much better."

"I don't deserve anything," she said. "What I want is a friend right now."

A friend. That's what he was to Jessa—what he always would be.

"I am your friend," he said.

"Good. Because I'm going to need my friends in the coming weeks as I make these changes." She studied him in the dimming daylight. "I'm scared, Will. I'm scared that I'm going to mess everything up again."

"You don't need to be scared, Jessa. You've got a whole

community to support you now. Those church ladies are your new best friends, whether you like it or not."

She smiled.

"And you've got me, too," he said, quieter. "I hope you don't mind."

"Mind?" She tilted her head. "I'm so thankful for you, Will. You've given me the hope I need to step out of what my life was and into what I want it to be. How could I mind?"

He nodded, his thoughts still on her news. She was leaving the resort. It was probably for the best—though, he would miss her more than ever.

"Do you want to get some supper?" he asked, suddenly needing to do something. If he only had a couple more weeks with her before she moved out, he needed to use the time wisely.

"What are you thinking?" she asked.

"How about the Drive-In?" He grinned. "It's probably been a while since you've been there."

"Ten years."

"Come on." He walked over to the sliding glass door and motioned for her to follow.

They locked the cabin and got into Will's car. The heaviness that had been hovering over them for the past week had lifted and though Will was sad that she was leaving, he felt hopeful for the first time in a long time that they could be friends, at least.

The Drive-In Restaurant, with a placard that said it was built in 1956, was on the south side of town, not too far from the old drive-in movie theater. The restaurant had retained its vintage charm through the years. Bright lights lit up the sign and the parking spots under the large canopy. Waiters and waitresses wore roller skates as they brought meals out to customers, and a line of cars, four deep, waited for a spot to park.

Will had always felt like he was going back in time when he ate there. Fifties and sixties music played on the speakers overhead, a pink 1950s convertible was permanently parked in the first stall, and the waitstaff was dressed in poodle skirts, cuffed jeans and white T-shirts. It was hard to visit the Drive-In and feel sad.

Thankfully, they didn't have long to wait before they pulled into a parking spot and Will pressed the call button on the order menu. The speaker was scratchy, but they were able to place their orders.

And they both ordered what they used to get in high school. A bacon cheeseburger, fries and a milkshake.

"I can't believe the Drive-In is still here," Jessa said as she settled back in the car and looked around at the restaurant. It was Saturday night, one of the busiest nights of the week.

"Timber Falls is one of a kind," Will said as he, too, took in the restaurant.

"Are you happy you came back?" Jessa asked him.

He smiled to himself. "I'm getting happier and happier each day."

"Oh?" She turned and looked at him. "Why?"

"If I hadn't come back, I wouldn't have been here when you needed me. And, more than that, you've helped me see Timber Falls in a new light. I have a lot more appreciation for this old town than I did a few weeks before you got here."

"I'm helping you appreciate it?" She shook her head and laughed. "My eighteen-year-old self didn't appreciate it at all."

"I don't think many eighteen-year-olds appreciate their

hometown. All they want to do is see the world—and rightfully so. But once you live in the real world for a while, you start to realize that no matter where you live, if you're not at peace with yourself, you won't be at peace with your surroundings. It's a hard lesson to learn, but almost all of us do."

"After some hard knocks."

"Of course." He smiled.

"Dream a Little Dream of Me" played over the loudspeakers and trickled into their vehicle. Nostalgia filled Will and for a second, he glanced over at Jessa.

Her cheeks were pink, and her hand was lying on her stomach. She was prettier to him than she'd ever been, and his heart filled with such longing, he thought it might burst.

There was so much he wanted to say—but something held him back. Jessa had a lot on her plate. The festival, a big move, a new baby and a new job. The last thing she needed was Will complicating things by telling her he was falling in love again. Especially when he didn't know how she felt.

A waitress brought out their meal and Will decided to leave the conversation alone.

They ate their meal, laughing and reminiscing about old memories from high school.

It felt good to forget about everything else for one night and to just breathe for a minute.

"I haven't had a bacon cheeseburger in years," Jessa said as she moaned in happiness. "I think the baby might start craving this after tonight."

Will grinned. "We know where to get another one, if we need to."

After they finished their meal, he pulled out of the restaurant, and they drove down Main Street. The Falls Theater was lit up and people were purchasing tickets at the sidewalk booth. The arts center was full, and a local comedian's name was on a poster in the front window. There was also a band in the park tonight.

"There's a lot going on," Will said to Jessa. "We could go to a movie, see the comedian or listen to the band. Do you feel like doing something fun?"

"I do," she said.

"Yeah? What would you like to do?"

"I want to go back to the resort and look at the stars."

Pleasure flooded Will and he smiled. "That sounds perfect."

"And it's free," she said with a laugh.

Will drove back to the resort and parked the car. The air had cooled since the sun went down, so Jessa went into her room to change, and Will grabbed a sweatshirt from his dresser.

They both entered the hallway at the same time—coming face-to-face.

It was quiet in the house and most of the lights were turned off.

For a second, they just looked at one another. Tension coiled around Will as he studied Jessa, wondering how she felt about him. She had left him—broken his heart. Did she regret her decision? Have second thoughts?

Jessa was wearing a pair of yoga pants and a thick cardigan. Her hair was up in a messy bun, and she looked adorable. He didn't even think she realized how cute she looked.

He wanted to reach out to her, pull her into his arms, but she held back, and he had remembered that she called him a friend.

If that's what Jessa Brooks needed, then that's what Will would remain.

A friend.

"Ready?" he asked.

She nodded and he indicated that she should proceed him out of the house.

They walked across the back lawn and down the steps to their dock.

How many times had they done this? And how many times would they do it again?

He didn't even want to think about it, because the truth was that these nighttime visits to stargaze were coming to an end. Once she moved to the condo, she'd never come back to look at the stars with him again.

The very thought made Will feel bereft.

Jessa had brought a blanket, which she laid on the dock.

"I might need help getting down and back up," she said with a giggle.

Will helped her down and then took a seat next to her—a little closer than he intended.

She wore a gentle perfume that he hadn't smelled since high school.

"What is that scent?" he asked.

Jessa lifted her wrist to his nose. "Don't you remember? You gave it to me for my birthday when I turned eighteen."

"I did?"

"I found it in my dresser earlier today and thought I'd put it on."

"I like it."

"I do, too." She smiled as she looked up at the stars overhead.

They were magnificent—something that never changed, even when everything else around him felt out of sorts.

"I feel like it's all coming to an end," Jessa said, quietly.

"What is?"

"My life before the baby. I was reading my mom's diary and she said that she lived twenty-four years before I was born but couldn't imagine life without me after I got here. I'll probably have the same feeling when my daughter is born."

Will nodded. He knew exactly how she felt.

Now that she was back, he couldn't imagine his life without Jessa, either.

Chapter Thirteen

The big day had finally arrived, and Jessa was a ball of nerves. She and Will arrived at Maple Island Park just as the sun was rising and met with the Riverfest planning committee members and volunteers. Already, there was activity in the park as different groups and organizations set up their tents and stations, preparing for the festival.

It wasn't easy to get around with her advanced pregnancy, so Jessa was thankful when one of the women from her mothers of preschoolers group arrived with a golf cart for her to use. Whitney Keelan was married to a golf professional, and they owned the local golf course. The cart became essential as Jessa was needed on one end of the park and then the other for hours before the festival even started.

Will was just as busy, helping people set up tents, directing traffic to designated spots and answering dozens of questions. When the electricity wasn't working for the food trucks, he was the one to call the power company to bring a technician to the park to deal with the problem. When two organizations were trying to set up their tents in the same space, he was the one to mitigate the issue and help relocate one organization.

And when Jessa realized she forgot her folder with all her notes, he ran back to the resort to get it for her.

Jessa couldn't have pulled off the festival without him.

Finally, at ten o'clock in the morning, the park was officially open, and the crowds began to descend.

For a few minutes, Jessa sat on the golf cart and just watched. This was her family's doing. This fun event, designed to bring the community together with family-friendly activities to celebrate the history of the river in Timber Falls, was because her grandparents had had a dream—one that was still rippling out for generations to enjoy. Would Jessa have that same kind of impact?

"Everything okay?" Will asked as he came up beside her.

He was wearing a simple pair of khaki shorts and a volunteer T-shirt, but he looked cute. His face was glowing, and he seemed to be a never-ending ball of energy.

"Volunteering looks good on you," Jessa said with a smile.

"Yeah?" He took a seat next to her on the golf cart. "Being a rock star leader looks good on you."

Her cheeks warmed. "I couldn't have done this without you," she said to him. "Thank you. If my grandparents and parents were here, they'd thank you, too."

He shrugged off her appreciation and looked at the festival.

The sparkling Mississippi River meandered through the park, offering a beautiful backdrop to the event. And just off to the right was the condo they had toured yesterday. Jessa's gaze landed there often, wondering what it would be like to live there, in such a pretty setting—away from Will.

"I'm proud of you, Jessa," Will said as he met her gaze. "Not a lot of people would have stepped in at the last minute like you did to take over the festival. If it hadn't been for you, none of these people would be here."

Jessa looked at the growing crowd. The laughing children, the smiling adults and the vendors who would benefit financially from the event.

"Timber Falls is blessed to have you back," he added.

Affection filled Jessa's heart and she smiled. "I'm blessed by Timber Falls."

He grinned. "Then it's a mutually beneficial relationship."

Jessa's cell phone rang, and she saw it was one of the committee members.

Soon, they were off fixing another problem.

By that evening, Jessa's feet and hands were swollen and her back ached. The excitement and energy she felt early in the day had waned and she was ready for bed. But the street dance was starting, and the fireworks would be shot off from the opposite side of the river at any minute. She had a few hours ahead of her before she could even think about going home.

Will had been called away to help the band set up their amplifiers and Jessa was trying to rest, as best as she could, on the golf cart. She had positioned herself near a willow tree with a great view of the river and the fireworks. The pavilion was to her right, offering a little privacy from the never-ending volunteers who had questions and problems.

Will had told her he'd join her as soon as he was able.

"Jessa!" a familiar voice said.

"Hello, Sandy." Jessa smiled at Will's mom and dad as they approached her. She started to get out of the golf cart, but Sandy held up her hand to stop her.

"Stay where you are, sweetheart," Sandy said. "You look exhausted."

"I am."

Sandy took Jessa's hand in her own. "You're swollen. Have you had enough water today? Are you dehydrated?"

Jessa held up her water bottle, thankful for Sandy's concern. "I'm hydrated."

"You should be at home with your feet up." She shook her head. "I don't like the looks of that swelling. If it doesn't go down tomorrow, you should go in and see your doctor."

"Tomorrow is Sunday."

"Go to urgent care, if you must."

"I have an appointment on Monday morning."

Sandy didn't look convinced, but she let go of Jessa's hand. "You'll do what's best."

Jessa nodded. She wasn't taking any chances.

"Everything went well today?" Jerry asked.

"By all accounts, yes." Jessa smiled. "I think everyone is very pleased with the turnout."

"You couldn't have had nicer weather," Jerry said.

"I agree." Jessa had been marveling at the weather all day. It was picture-perfect.

"We're going to visit some of the food trucks," Sandy said. "Have you eaten?"

"I've been nibbling all day—but I don't have much of an appetite. When you're done, come back and join us for the fireworks. Will is helping the band get set up, but he said he'd join me here to watch the display as soon as he can."

"We'll do that," Jerry said, rubbing his hands together. "But first, mini-doughnuts and cheese curds."

Sandy rolled her eyes playfully, but the sound of greasy mini-doughnuts and cheese curds made Jessa's stomach turn. Her head was starting to hurt, too. The idea of going home was more and more appealing.

"See you soon," Sandy said as they walked away from the golf cart and toward the food trucks. "Let us know if you need anything."

Jessa took a deep breath, trying to decide what she should

do. She was feeling crummier by the minute and wasn't sure if she would last through the fireworks. Maybe if she just closed her eyes and laid her head back for a few minutes to rest.

"There you are."

Jessa blinked her eyes open, and she realized she had fallen asleep.

Beck stood next to the golf cart, leaning against it as he watched Jessa.

"Oh," Jessa said, trying to get her bearings. She couldn't have been sleeping for long. But where was Will? He should have been there by now.

"Mind if I join you?" Beck asked as he slipped into the golf cart next to Jessa.

"Hey, Beck. I'm waiting for Will. He should be here any minute."

The first firework went off in the sky, drawing oohs and aahs from the crowd lined up on the banks of the Mississippi River.

"I wanted to let you know that everything is going well with the condo," Beck said. "You can move in as early as a week from this Monday. I'm working on all the paperwork, but the financial pieces have been settled. All that's needed is your signature on our loan agreement and you'll be set to go."

Jessa's head was pounding. "Can we talk about this Monday? I'm not feeling the best right now."

Another firework went off, sending bright pink sparkles into the air.

Where was Will?

"You okay?" Beck asked, looking concerned as he moved a little closer. He put his hand on her forehead, as if she was a child.

Jessa pulled back. "I'm not sick—it's been a long day and I'm exhausted. That's all."

Beck's arm went around her shoulders. "Can I do anything for you? Would you like me to take you home?"

Jessa moved forward, hoping he'd remove his arm, but he just followed her.

"Please, Beck," she said. "I just need some space."

He ran his hand over her cheek. "I only want to help."

She moved away from his hand, her stomach turning for more than one reason. "Can you find Will? I'd like him to take me home."

"Hey," Beck said as he gently touched her chin and directed her to look at him again. "I can take you home."

Before she knew what he was doing, Beck kissed her.

Jessa was stunned and it took her a moment to recover. She pulled back, horrified. "Why did you do that?"

"Isn't it obvious, Jessa? I'm in love with you. That's what all of this has been about."

Tears burned in Jessa's eyes, and she shook her head. "Please don't, Beck."

He stiffened. "You don't return my feelings?"

"No." She felt sicker than before and now she was crying.

Beck pulled back—and as he did, Jessa saw Will. He was standing at a distance, near the pavilion. Close enough to have seen Beck kiss her—but far enough away that he couldn't have heard their conversation.

"Will," Jessa called out to him, but he turned and walked away, getting swallowed by the crowd.

"Madden." Beck spit his name. "Is this because of him? Are you in love with him?"

Jessa hadn't told Will how she felt—so she wasn't about to tell Beck. But all thoughts vanished as the pain she'd been feeling in her back wrapped around her midsection, squeezing tight. It was so intense, she doubled over and gasped.

"Jessa?" Beck asked, concern in his voice. "What's wrong?"

"The baby," she managed to say through the pain. "I think something's wrong."

Beck jumped out of the golf cart and looked right and left. "What should I do?"

"Get Will," she said.

Nodding, Beck left without another word, probably relieved to leave her side and give this problem to someone else.

The pain gradually subsided, but the pounding in Jessa's head did not. It was ferocious.

She laid her forehead against the steering wheel and tried to take a deep breath.

"Jessa?" It was Sandy.

Relief overwhelmed Jessa. "It's the baby," she managed to say. "I think there's something wrong."

"Move over," Jerry instructed Jessa with no nonsense. "Sandy, get in on the other side. It'll be tight, but I'm driving you two to the hospital in the golf cart."

Jessa and Sandy did as instructed. Thankfully, the hospital was just a few blocks down the road. It would be faster than trying to find their car and maneuvering through the crowd of traffic that lined the street to watch the fireworks.

"Where is Will?" Jessa asked Sandy as they drove through the park, toward the road, with fireworks lighting up the sky.

"I don't know," Sandy said, her arm around Jessa. "I haven't seen him in hours."

"Can you try to call him?" she asked.

"Sure."

"Here's my phone." Jessa grabbed her cell phone out of the little holder.

Sandy tried calling Will, but he didn't answer—which was strange, since he'd had his phone with him all day.

It led Jessa to believe that he wasn't answering because it was her number—and he was upset about what he saw.

She didn't blame him. She was upset, too.

Will was so shaken up about Beck kissing Jessa that he hardly noticed anything as he pushed through the crowd toward his parked car.

Behind him, the fireworks blasted in the sky, lighting up the park, but that didn't even faze Will as he finally found his vehicle.

His phone started to ring, and he had a feeling it was Jessa. No doubt she felt like she had to explain what happened between her and Beck—but Will knew better. He had put his trust in her again and he had no one to blame but himself. Jessa hadn't made any promises to him—he didn't even know how she felt about him. If she wanted to kiss Beck Hanson, then who was he to stop her?

Yet, as he looked at the screen on his phone and saw Jessa's number, pain and anger sliced through him. What could she possibly say that would make him feel better right now? And was that even the reason she was calling? Did she care how he was feeling?

He turned off his cell phone and turned on his car engine. If Jessa and Beck were an item, Beck could drive Jessa home tonight. Will wasn't going to sit around and make a fool of himself any longer.

He pulled out of the parking lot and turned his car toward home. He'd been looking forward to watching the fireworks with Jessa, but now he wanted nothing to do with the fireworks or the festival.

It probably wasn't a great idea to drive when he felt this way. Everything was a blur as he drove through downtown Timber Falls. Thankfully, most people were at the park tonight, so the streets were empty.

When he finally pulled up to the cabin, he was breathing heavily. He still felt like someone had punched him in the gut—the same feeling he'd had when he read Jessa's letter ten years ago. As if he'd had the wind knocked out of him.

For a long time, he just sat in his car, staring at the cabin.

And it suddenly dawned on him why he had bought the resort.

He'd been trying to hold on to Jessa. To what they'd once had. He could claim it was for other reasons, but the truth was plain to see.

Now that she was with Beck, he felt like a fool. He'd never intended to own the resort to lure Jessa back—especially because he knew she had been married—but he had wanted to feel close to her. And he had, for a while.

He wouldn't accept a variance from Beck now, even if Beck begged him to accept it. Will was done with all of it. He wasn't going to hold on to the resort—not when Jessa was back in town and involved with his nemesis. He saw the folly of his ways and wasn't going to let Jessa have a hold on him any longer.

And he wasn't going to sit around and wait for her to come home tonight, either.

He bypassed the cabin and went to the boathouse where he'd been staying for the past few weeks. It wasn't a very big space, but it was comfortable. He flipped on the light and looked at the single room. A bed, a chair and a rug. All his clothes were still in his bedroom inside the cabin.

He sat on the chair and leaned forward, resting his elbows on his knees and his face in his hands. He had a lot of decisions to make—and the first was what he would do once he sold the resort.

Will wasn't sure how long he'd sat like that when he heard a knock at the door.

Was it Jessa? Had she come to try and explain herself?

He had no intention of listening, so he sat on the chair and tried to ignore her.

"Will?" a man asked from outside the door. "It's Beck. I need to talk to you. It's about Jessa."

Anger and jealousy surged through Will, and he was afraid of what he might do to Beck if he had to talk to him. "Go away, Beck. You're the last person I want to talk to."

"Jessa's at the hospital," Beck said, his voice muffled. "Something happened—"

Will was out of his chair and opening the door before Beck could finish his sentence. "What happened to Jessa?"

"I don't know. She asked me to find you and she called me from the hospital. They've admitted her because it looks like there's some complications. I've been calling your phone, but you didn't answer, so she told me to look for you here."

Will had left his phone in the car. He tore out of the boathouse and didn't wait for Beck to say more, but Beck kept up with him.

"I don't know what happened," Beck explained, "but she wasn't feeling good. I tried finding you at the festival, and when I couldn't locate you, I found one of the volunteers who had your cell phone number. I've tried calling you for the past thirty minutes."

Will continued to race across the lawn toward his car, wishing he hadn't left his phone. Was that why Jessa had tried to call him?

He felt horrible for not answering—for not being there for her when she needed him.

Without saying a word to Beck, Will got into his car—but at the last second, before closing the door, he said, "Thanks for finding me."

"I'd do anything for Jessa," Beck said. "No matter what's happened between you and me, it wasn't about that. It's always been about Jessa."

The vision of Beck kissing Jessa reared its ugly head and Will had to push down the jealousy again. Right now, Jessa needed him. It didn't matter where things stood between him and Beck.

"Are you coming to the hospital?" Will asked.

Beck shook his head. "I hate hospitals."

A dislike so strong and swift overtook Will and he had to force himself to close his car door and pull away from the resort. If Beck and Jessa were a couple, why wouldn't Beck want to be with her? Was he that selfish?

Will didn't care—all he could think about was getting to Jessa.

It was hard to go the speed limit, and he had to pass through downtown, which was now crowded with people trying to leave the park after the fireworks. Frustration mounted. He tried calling Jessa with his cell phone, but she didn't answer, which made him even more nervous.

He had missed fifteen calls and several texts. He couldn't check them while driving, but he was certain they were all from Jessa, Beck and his mom.

Finally, he pulled up to the hospital and found a place to park. It wasn't a good parking job, but all he could think about was Jessa. He ran across the parking lot and into the building.

A volunteer was sitting at the information desk, and he looked up with a pleasant smile.

"May I help you?" he asked.

Will was breathing hard. "I'm looking for my good friend Jessa Brooks. Can you help me find her?"

"Of course." The man pulled up Jessa's name on the computer screen and he nodded. "She's on the maternity floor. You can take the elevators up to floor four. Ask at the nurses' station for her room number—if she's receiving visitors. If she's not, they'll let you know what to do."

Will was already moving toward the elevator before the volunteer finished. He pressed the button and waited for a lifetime until the elevator doors opened.

A few minutes later, he stepped off the elevator and sprinted to the nurses' station.

He was still out of breath as he said, "Can you please tell me where I can find Jessa Brooks?"

The nurse looked up, a little surprised at his sudden appearance. "Is she expecting you?"

"I don't know." Will took several deep breaths. "She tried calling me, but when I called her back, she didn't answer. I'm afraid—" He couldn't finish that statement. There was so much he was afraid of.

"Let me check a few things and I'll get back to you." The nurse left the station and disappeared into a room. Was it Jessa's room?

Will paced across the floor—his heart in his throat.

Finally, the door opened, and the nurse came out, followed by Will's mom and dad.

Will stopped pacing, confused. "What are you guys doing here?"

"We were with Jessa at the festival when she went into

labor," Mom said as she gave Will a quick hug. "We brought her in."

"Labor?" Will asked. "She's having the baby? Isn't it too soon?"

"It's a little soon, but the doctor thinks the baby has a good chance—if there are no more complications or issues they aren't aware of." Mom's smile was tight. "We tried calling you several times. She asked for you."

"Can I see her?" he asked, looking toward the nurse.

The nurse nodded.

Will started to move away from his mom and dad, but his mom reached out and stopped him.

"She's scared, Will," Mom said. "She needs you to be strong for her."

"Of course." He would be anything and everything Jessa needed.

Mom smiled. "Good."

Will left them and entered the room.

Jessa was all alone on a bed, hooked up to several monitors that were beeping quietly. Her face was red, and she looked like she had been sweating.

She glanced up at his arrival and a dozen different emotions played out in her gaze—relief being foremost.

"You came," she said.

He walked across the room, his love for her propelling him. He didn't care if she didn't love him—all he cared about was making sure that Jessa and the baby were safe. Even if this wasn't the life God had for him, he would stand by Jessa's side—if she wanted him.

And he hoped she did.

Chapter Fourteen

Jessa had never been in so much pain in her life. It was hard to even comprehend. She had known it would hurt, but not this much. The contractions were coming about every five minutes, so she knew she had a little time before the next one.

But all she could think about was Will.

He reached her bed, and she lifted her hand, needing his strength.

"You came," she said again.

"Of course I came, Jessa. Nothing could have kept me from you."

"I thought you were mad at me, because of Beck—" She grimaced as another contraction started and she had to focus on breathing.

Will took her hand and put his other hand on her forehead. His palm was cool and gentle—nothing like Beck's had been. Even in the midst of her pain, she couldn't help but compare their touch and found Will's to be life-giving and reassuring.

"You're doing so well, Jessa," he said in a soothing voice.

Just feeling his touch and having him by her side relieved the tension that had twisted within her. Her contraction seemed more bearable with Will nearby.

She continued to focus on her breath and the pressure of his hands as the contraction passed.

"Thank you," Jessa said as she opened her eyes. His blue eyes were so full of concern—and was that love she saw?

Her heart tightened and the love she felt for him expanded. Did he still love her?

"What can I do for you?" he asked.

"Just be here," she said as she grasped his hand tighter. "Please don't leave me, Will. It seems bearable now that you're here."

"Are you sure?" he asked. "I have no idea what I'm doing."

"Neither do I—but the nurses have been great, and Dr. Smith will be here soon. All you need to do is stay."

"Of course I'll stay, Jessa. Always."

"Are you mad at me?"

"Shh," he said as he ran his hand over her forehead and moved her hair aside. "I'm not mad at you—but we can talk later. Right now, you just need to focus on bringing this baby into the world safe and sound. I'll do whatever you need me to do."

Jessa nodded as the door opened and Dr. Smith entered with one of the nurses who had helped to get her hooked up to the monitors.

"Hello, Jessa," Dr. Smith said. She smiled at Will. "It's nice to see both of you again."

"Is everything okay?" Will asked Dr. Smith.

Jessa had never seen him so uncertain.

"I'm about to check her," Dr. Smith said. "I don't have any major concerns right now, based on the nurse's report, but I need to have my own look." She studied Jessa. "Are you okay if I check everything?"

Jessa nodded.

"Do you want me to step out?" Will asked.

She held his hand tighter and shook her head. The idea of Will leaving the room, even for a second, made her feel almost panicked. She knew that giving birth wouldn't be glamorous, but she could think of no one in the world she'd rather have at her side.

Dr. Smith examined Jessa and asked her several questions about how she was feeling. When she finished, she smiled at Jessa.

"It looks like you're in active labor, which is what we assumed. The baby is a bit early, but not so early that I'm too concerned. She might need to stay in the hospital for a little longer than most babies, but if everything progresses as I expect it will, she should be here in a few hours. We'll try to make you as comfortable as possible, so let us know what you need. Okay?"

Jessa had had two contractions during the exam, and she was exhausted. "It's going to be several more hours?"

"It's hard to know for sure, but that's my best guess. The baby probably won't be born until tomorrow morning."

Dismay overwhelmed Jessa, but Will squeezed her hand with reassurance. "You've got this, Jessa. You're strong and courageous. I know you can do it."

Dr. Smith smiled at Will and nodded. Then she looked at Jessa. "The baby might surprise us and not take as long. You never know. But you're doing great, Jessa. Just keep breathing through the contractions and let your body do all the work. I'm heading home now, but I live close by. A nurse will let me know when you're ready to deliver and I'll hurry back."

The doctor was going home.

Jessa felt panicky until Will pulled a chair up to the side of the bed, reminding her that *he* was staying.

As the doctor and nurse left the room, Will smiled at

Jessa. He took her hand again and put his other hand on her cheek.

"Just think," he said, with awe in his voice, "in a few hours, you're going to hold your daughter for the first time and your life will never be the same again. Just a few hours."

"I'm so tired," Jessa said. "It's been such a long day."

"I know." He lifted her hand and kissed the back of it, his tenderness almost heartrending. "As soon as the baby is here, you can get some rest and I'll stay with her. I'm here for both of you."

Jessa nodded, pulling all her strength together as another contraction washed over her.

The hours seemed to drag as Jessa endured labor—but Will was by her side constantly. When she needed ice chips, he brought them, when she needed her brow wiped, he wiped it, and when she wanted the nurse, he ran to get her.

More importantly, he prayed for her and the baby.

Finally, around six in the morning, Dr. Smith returned and told Jessa it was time to start pushing.

Jessa had never been more exhausted in her life. She'd tried to rest between contractions, but it had been impossible.

Tears came to her eyes as she looked at Will, who had also sat up through the long night.

"I can't," she whispered.

"You can, Jessa," he said, smiling through his own tears. "She's almost here. You can do anything you set your mind to—and this is something your body was designed to do. You're going to do great."

His voice was reassuring and for some reason when he said she could, she felt like maybe she could.

The doctor and nurses set up the room for delivery and soon Jessa was pushing. It took another thirty minutes, but the baby was finally born and within seconds, she was crying.

Jessa lay back against the pillow, tears of joy, pain and relief streaming down her cheeks.

Will was also crying, and he looked at Jessa like she was the most amazing woman in the world—as if she was the first person to give birth to a child.

"You were incredible," he said as he kissed her brow. "I knew you could do it." He shook his head and lifted his shoulder to swipe away his tears. "That is the most miraculous thing I've ever seen."

"It's a beautiful, healthy little girl," Dr. Smith said as she held up the wailing baby.

Jessa's heart felt like it might burst at the sight of her daughter. She was tiny and absolutely perfect.

Dr. Smith laid the baby on Jessa's chest as the nurses cleaned her tiny body.

"Would you like to cut the cord?" Dr. Smith asked Will.

Will looked at Jessa, a question in his eyes.

She nodded.

Will did the honors.

Jessa's tears continued as she looked at her baby's beautiful face, her tiny fingers, her fingernails and the silky black hair on her little head.

"She's gorgeous," Will said as he, too, inspected the baby. "Look at how perfect everything is."

"We'll get her cleaned up, weighed and measured, and bring her back to you," a nurse said.

Jessa nodded, feeling a loss when they took the baby out of her arms.

It took a bit of time to care for both Jessa and the baby, but when all was put to rights, Dr. Smith brought the baby back to Jessa, wrapped in a pink blanket.

"She's perfect," Dr. Smith said. "A little small at five pounds, two ounces, but her lungs are strong, her heart is beating well and she's responding as expected. Congratulations, Jessa."

"Thank you," Jessa said as she took the baby from Dr. Smith.

"Be sure to call the nurses if you need anything," the doctor said. "I'll be doing my rounds this morning and come back before I leave for home this afternoon to check on you."

"Thank you," Jessa said again. "I'm so grateful for all your help."

"My pleasure." Dr. Smith patted Jessa's leg and then squeezed Will's forearm before she left the room.

Soon, the nurses followed.

Sunshine poured into the room and Jessa glanced at the clock. It was already after eight.

Will smiled down at Jessa and the baby, shaking his head. "I had no idea."

"What?" she asked.

"The whole thing. Labor, delivery—seeing her for the first time."

"Would you like to hold her?" Jessa asked.

Will looked from the baby to Jessa. "Is that okay?"

Jessa smiled and nodded. "Of course."

She lifted the baby and Will gently took her into his arms.

The look of awe on his face made Jessa's tears return and she knew she'd never forget it. Every baby girl deserved a daddy to look at her the way Will was looking at her now—except, Will wasn't the daddy, as much as Jessa wished he was.

Will lifted the baby and kissed her forehead. "What will you call her?"

"I want to give a nod to her French heritage, since she probably won't have any other connection to that side of her family, and name her Cosette."

"Cosette?" Will's voice was sweet and loving. "It's perfect." He glanced up at Jessa. "Will you tell her father?"

Sadness filled Jessa and she shook her head. "Philippe made it very clear he had no wish to ever hear from me again. As far as I'm concerned, Cosette doesn't have a father."

The truth of it hit hard.

A knock at the door brought both of their heads up.

"Hello?" came Sandy's voice. "May we come in?"

"Yes," Jessa said, wiping the tears from her face. "Come in."

Sandy and Jerry entered the room with a large bouquet of flowers and a balloon that said It's a Girl.

"Congratulations," Sandy said as she smiled at Jessa. Her gaze traveled to her son, who was holding Cosette, and she pressed her lips together as tears filled her eyes. "There she is."

Jerry was behind Sandy, a smile on his face, though he didn't seem as eager as Sandy to see the baby.

"Her name is Cosette," Will said. "Would you like to hold her?"

"Of course," Sandy said. "That's why we came."

Will handed Cosette to Sandy and Jessa watched with quiet thankfulness.

Maybe Cosette wouldn't have a dad—or grandparents—but she was thankful for Will and the Maddens, who had stepped in to fill those places in Cosette's life—even if for just today.

Will was exhausted, but he'd had a surge of energy since Cosette had made her appearance. Watching Jessa bring life into the world was one of the most profound things he'd ever witnessed. His respect and admiration for her had grown in leaps and bounds.

As his mom held Cosette, Will turned to Jessa. She looked worn out, but she was glowing, and when she met his gaze, he realized that their bond had strengthened exponentially. How could it not? He loved her, deeply, and loved her more for what he had just witnessed. The depth of her sacrifice for her child, and the way in which she had given everything she had, made her one of the most beautiful women he'd ever beheld.

"I'm so proud of you," he said to Jessa, knowing that the love he felt for her was evident in his voice and his gaze. Yet—he couldn't tell her. Not now, not when she was so exhausted and overwhelmed. His own emotions were frayed.

But, could he ever tell her? What if she and Beck had come to some sort of arrangement? Just thinking about them kissing in the park last night made all the anger and jealousy rise to the surface again. He hated feeling that way and wasn't willing to take the risk in offering his heart to Jessa when he didn't know how she felt about him.

He tore his gaze from her, needing a little space to sort out his feelings.

"I'm going to grab some coffee," he said, knowing his parents would keep Jessa company. "Anyone want anything?"

His mom hardly heard him as she was oohing and aahing over the baby, and his dad shook his head. When he looked back at Jessa, there was sadness in her gaze, but she said no.

Will left the room and took a deep breath. The past twelve hours had been some of the most emotional he'd ever endured. What he needed was sleep and some distance from Jessa and the baby. It was all too much. He couldn't trust his heart right now.

The nurses told him there was coffee in the waiting room, so he went in that direction and poured himself a cup. But he didn't drink it right away—instead, he stood at the large floor-to-ceiling window and looked out at the parking lot and the green lawn beyond.

Vehicles drove up and down Main Street and people were coming and going from the hospital and the other buildings nearby. The sun was shining bright, and the world looked so promising. But, for Will, it was uncertain and dim. What would he do without Jessa now that he had spent the past few weeks with her again? Fallen in love and allowed himself the luxury of imagining a life with her? And how would he tell her he was going to sell the resort, because he couldn't keep it after everything that had happened?

"Will?"

He turned and found his mom and dad entering the waiting room, concern mounting. She shouldn't have to be alone after all she'd been through. "Why'd you leave Jessa?"

"It was time for her to feed the baby," Sandy said. "The nurses shooed us out of her room."

"Oh." Will let out a sigh and leaned against the steel window frame, scolding himself for being so protective of her.

"Come have a seat," Mom said as she wrapped her arm through Will's and led him to one of the couches. "We need to talk."

"I don't like the sound of that," Will said. Even though he was twenty-eight, his mom still had the ability to make him feel like a willful five-year-old.

"You probably won't like it," she said. "But I need to say it."

Jerry scratched behind his ear and looked toward the door. "I, uh, think I'll go wait in the car."

Mom waved him off, as she often had when dealing with Will and Allison through the years.

Will set his coffee on the table and faced his mom. "What?"

"What are you doing with that young woman in there?" she asked.

Frowning, Will shook his head. "What are you talking about?"

"It's obvious to anyone with eyes that you're still in love with her." She studied him. "So, what are you going to do about it?"

"Weren't you the one who told me to be careful with Jessa? To keep her at a distance?"

Mom frowned. "No. If I remember correctly, I just told you I was worried about you and that it was going to be impossible for you to not get your heart involved with Jessa again. And I was right, wasn't I?"

He looked down at the ground, unable to deny her assessment.

"I didn't tell you to keep your distance," she continued. "I knew you'd fall for her again and I was a little upset that she put you in that position. But you were quick to point out that she was desperate—and you were right. She did need you. I believe God placed you in the right spot at the right time to be His hands and feet in Jessa's life. She didn't come back to hurt you or to manipulate you or to use you."

"What did you want to talk to me about?" She hadn't told him anything he didn't already know.

"If you love Jessa," Mom said, leveling him with a look, "then tell her and stop moaning about, afraid of taking a risk."

He leaned forward, his elbows on his knees, and put his face in his hands. "I have no idea how she feels."

"Are you blind, William Thomas Madden?" she asked. "That girl is crazy for you. It's written all over her face. But she's just as scared as you to say something. She knows she hurt you in the past and she doesn't want to hurt you again. She's afraid if she says something, and you don't return her feelings, then she'll lose you forever."

Will slowly sat up straight to look at his mom. "You think she still loves me?"

"I do." Mom smiled. "You two were perfect together when you were in high school, and it was only immaturity and inexperience that drove you apart. Now that you have some wisdom and you're both in a position to enter a relationship, I believe it will be better than ever. Yes, there is heartbreak and pain in your past, but that will only make you stronger, if you let it."

She put her hands on either side of his face. "But if you're not ready to commit to Jessa and that baby, don't tell her how you feel." She lowered her hands. "They need stability, protection and comfort right now. Jessa is still reeling from the trauma she experienced, but I can see her wounds are already healing because of you. She trusts you, Will. If you are ready to accept the responsibility of her trust, then run to her. If not, let her go."

"I would do anything within my power to protect her and Cosette," he said.

"Good. After what Jessa has been through, she needs someone who is willing to be her defense against the world." Mom smiled. "I know you have it within you to be a wonderful husband and father. All you need to do is take the risk and tell Jessa how you feel."

Will's heart was pumping hard at the thought. If his mom

was right, he would be the happiest man alive. If she was wrong, it would destroy him. Because as confident as she sounded, Will couldn't be so sure. He wanted to believe it was true, but he'd had enough heartbreak to know things weren't always as they seemed.

"Do you think I should talk to her now?" he asked. "We're both exhausted and emotional."

"Don't waste another second, Will. She and Cosette are worth the risk."

His mom was right. Jessa and Cosette were worth any risk he would ever take.

Will hugged his mom and she hugged him back. "I love you," he said.

"I love you, too, kiddo." She pulled back and smiled. "Now go tell Jessa how you feel."

He took a deep, steadying breath and then stood and walked across the waiting room.

As he followed the hallway back to Jessa's room, he couldn't remember a time when he felt this nervous or certain that his life was about to change. Whether for good or bad, he wasn't sure, but he knew he wouldn't walk out of the hospital room the same man he walked in.

He lightly knocked on the door, but no one answered, so he pushed it open.

The room was quiet, and the shades had been drawn, creating a semidarkness. Jessa was in the bed and Cosette was in the clear bassinet nearby.

Both were sound asleep.

Will walked over to the bassinet and looked down at the baby. Her lips were puckered into a perfect little circle as she slumbered. She was beautiful—perfection in a little human form.

And then Will looked at Cosette's mama. Her dark hair

was in a braid, which lay on her shoulder. Though she was sleeping, exhaustion still lined her face. She had worked hard, after a long day, and she needed all the sleep she could get.

Will didn't want to wake her or the baby. What he had to say could wait until she was rested and in a better frame of mind.

And there was still the matter of Beck. Had that kiss been mutual? Had Jessa invited it? Will had come around the corner right as the kiss had started and looked away as soon as he realized what was happening.

Maybe he had overreacted. Maybe it had been all Beck's doing.

The last thing Will wanted to do was cause Jessa distress. He would let her sleep and then he'd come back a little later, after he had some rest, too, and they could talk.

He just hoped Beck wouldn't beat him to it—or make Jessa another offer she couldn't refuse.

Chapter Fifteen

A strange sound broke into Jessa's dream, and she frowned. Her eyes were so heavy, it took all her effort to open them. But when she did, she blinked a few times, trying to make sense of where she was.

And then the sound came again, wrapping around Jessa's heart like a ribbon, wending its way into her very soul.

It was her daughter.

Cosette's cry was the sweetest thing Jessa had ever heard.

"What's wrong, little one?" she asked as she leaned over and put her hand on Cosette's soft, pink cheek. "Mama's here."

Cosette's cries stopped for a heartbeat at the sound of Jessa's voice, and she started moving her face toward Jessa's hand.

"Are you hungry?" she asked the baby, knowing full well that a newborn was always hungry. She'd read a few books in preparation for the birth of her daughter and the lactation consultant had been in earlier when Sandy and Jerry had been visiting. But head knowledge was different from experience, and Jessa was a little nervous. What if she didn't know how to feed her own baby by herself?

Slowly, Jessa lifted Cosette out of her bassinet, amazed all over again about how small she was, and positioned herself to feed the baby.

It took a little practice, but eventually the two of them figured it out and Cosette's cries stopped.

The room was quiet and dim from the shades over the windows. Jessa looked at the clock and saw it was a few minutes before noon. She hadn't been sleeping long—maybe three hours. But even three hours felt better than nothing.

She yawned and looked at the beautiful flowers from the Maddens—and then she remembered Will. He'd gone out for coffee. Had he come back to find her asleep? Had he left the hospital?

More importantly, would he be back?

Uncertainty filled her heart as she returned her gaze to Cosette. No doubt Will was as exhausted as her. Had he gone to the cabin to sleep?

She didn't want to call him in case he was sleeping. But then she realized that it was Sunday and there were guests checking out of the resort. He was probably working—and not sleeping, like he needed.

She tried not to worry that he wasn't coming back. He'd been so patient and steadfast through her entire labor and delivery, he wouldn't leave them now, would he? He didn't owe her anything, but she hoped he wanted to come back.

As the day progressed, Jessa was able to take naps in between feedings and visits from the doctor and nurses. She was able to get up and take a shower, have a good meal and feel a little more refreshed.

Just after three o'clock, her phone dinged, indicating a text.

Hey, Jessa. I hope you've had a chance to sleep. Do you need anything from home?

Those three simple sentences felt life-giving and brought hope to her heart.

Will was coming back—and he wanted to know if she needed anything from home.

Home.

The resort was and always would be home, even if she didn't live there. She had so many decisions to make, but she decided to give herself a little break and not worry about them today.

Today was all about Cosette.

She started typing her response.

I've had some good sleep and a shower, but I need my hospital bag. I packed it a couple days ago. It's on the floor, next to my bed. Thank you.

Turning off her phone, she set it aside, wondering when he might come.

They'd been through a lot together, but experiencing the birth of her child, with Will by her side, had taken the love she felt for him and grown it beyond anything she had imagined. How could she love someone so much? And how would she go on with her life without being able to tell him? He'd never trust her again—would he? Especially after seeing Beck kiss her.

Just thinking about Beck's kiss made Jessa groan. She hadn't thought about it until now, and wished she could forget about it.

A knock at her door sent Jessa's heart pounding, but she realized it couldn't possibly be Will—not if he had texted her from the cabin.

"Come in," she called.

It was as if she had brought Beck to her door by thinking about him.

He entered with a huge bouquet that put the Maddens' to shame, and half a dozen balloons.

"Congratulations," he said as he set his gift on the counter.

She was in the gown and robe the hospital provided, and was fully clothed, but she still felt vulnerable and uncomfortable in his presence. Especially after last night's kiss.

"Hello, Beck."

"Wow." Beck walked up to the bassinet where Cosette was sleeping. "She's beautiful."

"Thank you."

"Looks like her mom."

"Thank you," Jessa said again, and then asked, "What are you doing here, Beck?"

"I came to congratulate you."

She took a deep breath, not feeling emotionally ready for this talk, but it was time they had it—especially after he kissed her.

"I think it's best if you leave," she said. "I appreciate the flowers and the gesture—but after last night, I'd like to put some distance between us."

"Because I kissed you?" He scoffed. "Don't be juvenile, Jessa. It was a simple kiss."

"No—not to me. It was a violation of my personal space and my trust."

"What does that mean?"

"It means that if I can't trust you, then I can't work for you." She knew what she was risking, Will's variance, but she also knew that she could no longer put herself in positions to be hurt or worse. She had a child to think of now and no matter how much she loved Will, she had to be the best version of herself for Cosette.

"You're not going to work for me?" Beck asked. "Even at the risk of Madden losing his variance?"

"Yes." She lifted her chin. "I want Will to get the variance, more than almost anything else, but I must think about what's best for Cosette now. And I've spent too many years being afraid and vulnerable. I can't put myself in that position with you."

He looked down at the sunglasses he was holding and didn't speak for a few moments.

Jessa waited, afraid of what he might say.

But when he looked up at her, she saw remorse in Beck's gaze.

"I'm sorry, Jessa. Yesterday I told Madden that I would do anything for you and that's the truth. I do want you to work for me, but if it makes you uncomfortable, then I'd hate myself."

She stared at him, surprised at his response.

"I want what's best for you, too," he continued. "And if it's not me, then I'll have to bow out. I'd like to step away with a little self-respect, so I'll stop bothering you."

"Thank you," she said. "I would like to be friends, if possible."

"Sure." He offered a half-hearted smile and Jessa knew that they would never be friends.

He probably knew it, too.

"I'll put a halt on the condo purchase," he said. "I'm sure you'd rather live at the resort anyway."

She looked down at her hands, not wanting to reveal her heart to Beck.

"Bye, Jessa. I wish you well."

"Bye."

He walked out of the hospital with his head high and as the door closed, Jessa breathed a sigh of relief, thanking God that the conversation had gone better than she could hope.

And Will hadn't come upon them, making it more awkward.

Cosette began to fuss, so Jessa got up and changed her, then took her to the rocking chair and began to feed her.

When she was finished, Jessa just held her, rocking back and forth, and began to hum a gentle lullaby that her father had sung to her when she was small.

A knock at the door brought Jessa's head up and her heart began to beat hard.

"Come in," she said.

Will entered the room, her bag in one hand and a beautiful bouquet of wildflowers that looked like they'd come from the riverbank in the other. He'd also showered and changed out of the Riverfest volunteer T-shirt he'd been wearing yesterday. He looked handsome in a button-down shirt and pair of shorts. And when their gazes met, the gentle smile he gave her caused butterflies to fill her stomach.

She knew her heart was in her gaze, and she couldn't hide her feelings any longer. She loved him and didn't care if he knew. Giving birth to her daughter had caused a surge of courage she didn't know she had, and she was willing to deal with whatever may come.

Without a word, Will set her bag and the flowers on the counter and walked across the dim room to where she sat.

He bent down on one knee and placed a kiss on Cosette's head before looking up at Jessa.

"Hi," he said.

"Hi."

"How are you feeling?"

"Better," she said with a smile, amazed at how much he lifted her spirits. "Thank you for the flowers."

His smile was sweet as he studied her, as if looking for answers to a question. Was it the same question beating in her heart?

"I saw Beck when I got here," he said. "He was just leaving."

Jessa looked at the large bouquet and balloons, causing Will to glance in that direction. When he returned his gaze to her, his eyes didn't hold the anger they usually did when talking about Beck.

"He told me what you said." Will continued to study her.

"I turned down his offer—even if it means—"

"I don't get my variance."

Jessa nodded, afraid that she had hurt him.

But the look in his eyes was the opposite of hurt. He looked very pleased.

"Thank you for making a choice for you, Jessa—that makes me happier than all the variances in the world."

A slow smile tilted her lips. "Really?"

"Really."

He laid his hand on Cosette's little body and smiled as he looked from the baby to Jessa.

"I was thinking," he said, "that this puts you and Cosette in a hard place."

"We'll figure things out," Jessa said, a little breathless.

"What would you say if I volunteered to help you figure it out?"

"What do you have in mind?"

He took her free hand in his and lifted it to his lips. Gently, and with great care, he placed a kiss on the top of her hand. "I'm wondering if you and Cosette would like to stay at the resort—for good."

She pressed her lips together, waiting.

"And if you would like a husband and if Cosette would like a daddy."

Tears filled Jessa's eyes and she had to swallow before she could answer. "We would."

A bright smile filled Will's face. "Really?"

"Really."

"And are you okay if that husband and daddy is me?"

"You're the only one I want."

He put his hand on her cheek and placed a kiss on her lips—it was gentle and achingly tender, filled with years of brokenness and healing.

When he pulled back, he whispered, "I love you, Jessa."

"I love you, too, Will."

"And I love Cosette," he said, "with all of my heart."

Jessa's own heart felt like it might burst from joy, and she could almost imagine her dad smiling at them.

"We're going to be very happy," she whispered.

"The happiest."

Jessa couldn't wait.

The weather wasn't quite what Will had hoped for on his wedding day, but at least the rain seemed to be holding off. An outdoor wedding, near the banks of the Mississippi River, had seemed like a great plan when he and Jessa were discussing it—but the clouds were a little daunting. At least it kept the heat at bay and offered a little respite from the sun that had been blazing down all week. They'd also had the forethought to rent a large white tent, which their guests were sitting under as they waited for the ceremony to begin.

Will stood near the steps leading down to the dock where he and Jessa had spent so many hours gazing at the stars. His chest filled with anticipation of all the stargazing yet to come. The past four weeks had gone by in a happy blur as they had adjusted to life with Cosette and planned their wedding. Will had stayed in the boathouse and Jessa and Cosette had lived in the cabin where Jessa had sorted and organized Cosette's bedroom. His mom and dad had been over often to help with the baby and do what they could for the wedding plans. Jessa loved having his mother's help and thrived on her experience and wisdom.

Now, as Will waited for Jessa to come out of the cabin and join him near the steps, his heart was pounding hard.

They had decided to keep the wedding small and intimate with only their closest friends and Will's family. Allison had come home and was Jessa's maid of honor, while Will had asked his friend Max Evans to be his best man. They had invited a few of their church friends and the church ladies had offered to make a light lunch, which they would enjoy under the tent when the ceremony was over.

Everything had been simple, since there wasn't a lot of money, though Will's parents had given them some and the church ladies insisted on putting on the meal.

But none of it mattered to him or Jessa. They wanted to be married and to start their lives as husband and wife. The rest was just extra.

The violinist began to play "Canon in D" as the sliding glass door opened and Will's mom appeared, holding little Cosette.

He grinned at the sight of his daughter, just four weeks old. She was wearing an adorable white dress that his mom had bought for her. His mom glowed as she walked down the aisle and took a seat at the front. She smiled at Will, her happiness just as keen as the rest of them.

Next came Allison, holding a small bouquet of roses. She was smiling, too, and Will could see she was fighting back tears. When they had told her they were getting married and Jessa wanted her as the maid of honor, Allison had been ridiculously happy. She'd told them she had known it all along and wasn't surprised.

When Allison got to the front of the tent, she winked at Will before taking her place.

"Will everyone rise for the bride?" Pastor Jake asked.

Everyone stood as Jessa appeared at the open door. She looked stunning in a beautiful white dress. It was simple, with no frills or ruffles or lace. Just white satin. She wore her dark hair up and had a pretty clip tucked into the side, but there was no veil. She also carried a bouquet of red roses, and they looked brilliant against her white dress.

At her side was Will's dad. He had asked Jessa if he could walk her down the aisle and she had cried tears of joy.

When Will's gaze met Jessa's, he realized that he hadn't understood true love or happiness until that very moment. All the hopes and dreams he had for the future were bound together with his love for Jessa and Cosette. All that he was and all that he had, he would offer to them, though he feared it would never be enough.

Jessa and his dad moved down the aisle, but Jessa never once looked away from Will.

And he knew, because he didn't look at anyone else but her.

When they finally arrived at the front, Will's dad placed Jessa's hand into Will's and squeezed them both for a split second before taking a seat with Will's mom.

"Who gives this woman to be married to this man?" Pastor Jake asked.

"I give myself," Jessa said with a tender smile, "and I know my father would, too, if he were here today."

Will's chest expanded at the knowledge, and he nodded. Oliver Brooks would be a very happy man if he knew Jessa and Will were getting married. In his heart of hearts, Will suspected that Oliver always believed it would happen. Somehow. Someway.

"Dearly beloved," Pastor Jake began, "we gather here today to witness the marriage of William Madden and Jessa Brooks. This contract of marriage is not to be entered into lightly, but thoughtfully and respectfully, with a deep understanding of its obligations and responsibilities. Marriage is a commitment of love, loyalty and trust. It is with this intention that we proceed."

Will could think of nothing but Jessa by his side. She squeezed his hand and he looked at her, unable to believe that this was really happening, after so much time and heartache. Yet—it was because of that pain that he knew such joy now. He did not enter this union lightly or without great thought.

Pastor Jake continued to speak, and Will tried to listen, but his heart and mind were full of so many thoughts and feelings, it was hard to concentrate.

Finally, Pastor Jake said, "May I have the rings?"

Max handed the rings to Pastor Jake, and he prayed over them, blessing them, before handing the rings to Will and Jessa.

"Repeat after me," he said to Will first.

And Will did, saying, "Jessa, with this ring, I take thee to be my wedded wife, to have and to hold, from this day forward, for better, for worse, for richer, for poorer, in sickness and in health, to love and to cherish, till death do us part, according to God's holy ordinance, and thereto I pledge myself to you."

He slipped the simple gold band on Jessa's left ring finger and smiled at her as tears glistened in her eyes.

"Now, Jessa," Pastor Jake said, "take Will's ring and repeat after me."

Jessa did the same, saying, "Will, with this ring, I take thee to be my wedded husband, to have and to hold, from this day forward, for better, for worse, for richer, for poorer, in sickness and in health, to love and to cherish, till death do us part, according to God's holy ordinance, and thereto I pledge myself to you."

The ring was warm as Jessa slid it onto Will's finger, sealing their love and commitment.

"Now, by the authority vested in me by Almighty God and the state of Minnesota, I pronounce you husband and wife. What God has brought together, let no man put asunder. Amen." He winked at Will. "You may kiss your bride."

Will grinned as he took Jessa in his arms and kissed her in front of their friends and family.

Everyone cheered and rose to their feet.

Will pulled away, his pulse thumping hard, and looked at his bride.

"My wife," he said.

"My husband," she responded.

"I love you, Jessa."

"I love you, too, Will."

His mom approached with Cosette and placed the baby in Will's arms and then they faced the audience and received more applause.

They were finally a family, complete and whole.

The guests were so few that they were able to stop at each one and receive well-wishes as they greeted them individually. Many of them oohed and aahed over Cosette, who had slept through her parents' wedding.

When all the chairs were moved aside and the tables

were being set up for the meal, Will handed Cosette off to his mom and took Jessa by the hand.

"I want a few minutes alone with my wife," he told her as he drew her away from the crowd and around to the front of the cabin.

There, he kissed her again, and this time, without an audience.

She was sweet and eager as she returned his kiss.

"No more sleeping in the boathouse," he told her.

"Not anymore," she agreed with a smile.

He held her in his arms, reveling in her nearness and the newness of their union.

"Would it be rude to tell everyone to go home so I can be alone with my wife?" he asked.

"Yes."

He laughed. "I thought so."

A car turned off the main road and into the resort.

Will moaned. "It's Beck. If he came to stop this wedding, he's too late."

Jessa pulled out of Will's embrace, but stayed by his side as Beck parked his car and got out.

"I'm assuming congratulations are in order?" Beck asked as he walked up to them.

"You're looking at the new Mr. and Mrs. Madden," Jessa said to him.

"Then, congratulations," Beck said as he offered Will his hand. "It looks like the best man won."

Will stared at Beck's hand for a second and then shook it. "Thanks."

"And you look beautiful, Jessa," Beck said.

"Thank you."

"What brings you here today?" Will asked. "I hope you weren't planning to stop the wedding."

"Of course not." Beck pulled an envelope from inside his suit coat and handed it over to Will. "Let's call this a wedding present."

Will removed his arm from around Jessa and took the envelope. He stared at it for a second before opening it.

"What is it?" Jessa asked.

"It's the variance to build the amusement park," Will said, a little surprised as he looked from the variance to Beck. "Is this for real?"

"It's the real deal," Beck said. "The city council approved it at our Monday night meeting, but I held on to it until today to give to you for a wedding gift."

Will was speechless. He hadn't even known that Beck had brought it before the city council. His emotions overwhelmed him. For the past four weeks, he and Jessa had been trying to think of ways to keep the resort going. They had finally come to terms with the fact that Will would need to find a job to help support them, though it wouldn't be easy to work full-time and run the resort.

Now, he wouldn't have to.

"Thank you," Will said as he slipped the variance back into the envelope. "I can't tell you how much this means to me."

"And to me," Jessa said.

"We're both thankful," Will continued.

"Well, when it's a success, as I know it will be," Beck said, "make sure you give me the credit for believing in your dreams."

Will wanted to roll his eyes, but he saw that Beck was trying to ease the tension of the moment.

So Will stuck out his hand again and Beck took it.

"I wish you both the best," Beck said.

"Would you like to stay for lunch?" Jessa asked. "There's plenty."

"No, thanks." He started to walk away and said over his shoulder, "I have a date."

He waved as he pulled out of the parking lot and Will turned to Jessa, still a little incredulous.

"Look at that," Will said to his wife. "Two dreams come true on the same day."

"Which two?" she asked.

"I got to marry you and I have the variance to build the theme park."

Jessa smiled as she lifted her face for him to kiss her again. "And it's just the beginning."

Will kissed his wife and couldn't help but marvel at the gifts God had given him. A wife, a baby and a home to grow old in together.

* * * * *

*If you liked this story from Gabrielle Meyer,
check out her previous Love Inspired books:*

A Mother's Secret
Unexpected Christmas Joy
A Home for Her Baby
Snowed in for Christmas
Fatherhood Lessons
The Soldier's Baby Promise
The Baby Proposal
The Baby Secret

*Available now from Love Inspired!
Find more great reads at www.LoveInspired.com.*

Dear Reader,

I love summertime in central Minnesota. It makes living through the long winters worth the wait! It's fun to share my love for my home state through the stories I write. I enjoyed creating the fictional resort where Jessa grew up, since it reminds me of several resorts I've visited over the years. Little cabins, campfires, boating and laughter create some of the best memories for both children and adults. My hope is that you felt like you were there with Will and Jessa, if only for a little while.

Blessings,
Gabrielle Meyer